A WITCH FOR MR. MISTLETOE

WITCHES OF CHRISTMAS GROVE
BOOK FOUR

DEANNA CHASE

D1603081

ABOUT THIS BOOK

A small town paranormal romance

Olivia Mann has started over. After a rough divorce, she's back in Christmas Grove with her dream job of running an enchanted inn. This season she's hosting the cast of a popular television show while they film a holiday special. Everything is looking up, until her chef has an accident and is out of commission for three months. After struggling to find a replacement, she has no choice but to hire Declan McCabe... the man she hoped to never see again.

Declan McCabe is between jobs. His plan was to take a long vacation before starting his new five-star job in the city. But when his sister breaks her leg, he's strongarmed into helping her out. He's now the head chef at The Enchanted, a magical inn on the outskirts of Christmas Grove. The inn itself is full of spelled surprises and a handful of charming spirits. The only problem is his new boss, Olivia Mann. She's both beautiful and the most irritating person he's ever met… until she isn't. All he wants to do is finish his time in Christmas Grove and move on, but when mistletoe is involved, suddenly he finds himself kissing the one woman he shouldn't. And now Christmas Grove is starting to get into his bones. He's going to need a little Christmas magic if he's going to get the happily-ever-after he didn't know he wanted.

CHAPTER 1

"Water, Scooter, no!" the blond PA wearing jeans and a puffy down jacket called as she chased a brindle-colored and a gold-and-white shih tzu right past the reception desk and straight into the kitchen.

A loud crash sounded, followed by a cranky chef's bellow. "Get out of my kitchen! Now!"

Olivia, the owner of the inn, winced as she craned her neck to try to see the destruction through the open door. Red sauce was splattered across the floor. "Oh no," she breathed, praying that neither of the prized dogs were hurt. Clutching her phone, she tightened her grip and willed that the woman on the other end of the line would finally find her credit card so that they could finish the reservation.

The door swung open and Tracy, the PA, stumbled backward, nearly losing her balance as she gave Olivia a helpless stare. She and an entire Hollywood crew were on location at Olivia's inn, filming for the next few months.

While the inn wasn't big enough for everyone to stay there, the production company had rented rooms for the principal actors for the duration of the film so that they were never far should the filming times change. "I'm so sorry," she said, pressing a hand to her stomach. "I don't know how they got out of Priscilla's room."

Priscilla was the star of the holiday movie, *Merry Me for Christmas,* and was more than a prima donna. When she found out her babies were on the loose, heads would roll. No doubt the PA was going to be in serious trouble even if this was in no way her fault.

The woman on the other end of the phone finally let out a sigh of relief. "Got it!"

Olivia quickly finished up the reservation and by the time she ended the call, Tracy's face was white as she paced in front of the kitchen door, nervously chewing on one of her thumbs.

What in the fresh mistletoe was the PA doing? Had she really left those dogs in the kitchen with Declan McCabe, a chef who was such a stickler for health regulations that he'd already fired two people for minor infractions? One for using the beef spatula on a chicken dish and another for using an ingredient a day after its expiration date. The very idea that dogs were in his kitchen was unthinkable.

How was it possible he wasn't already bellowing Olivia's name?

The fact that there was no sound at all coming from the kitchen worried her the most. Olivia ignored the PA and burst into the kitchen, finding it completely empty.

"Declan?" she called out, pleased there wasn't an ounce

of panic in her tone. The PA wasn't the only one who'd pay for the escaped dogs. Olivia just couldn't afford for anything to go wrong. Not when she'd sunk every last dollar she had into The Enchanted. The income this movie would provide was what was going to get her through her first year as a proprietor of the inn. "Declan, are you here?"

Still no answer.

Frowning, Olivia carefully walked past the tomato-based sauce and poked her head into the dry goods storage room. No Declan. No dogs.

"You're okay, sweetheart," Declan's gentle voice filtered in from the window.

Olivia climbed up on the stepstool and peeked out the small window. Declan was crouched down on the patio, holding Scooter as he rinsed her coat with the hose, while Tater tried her best to rip his pant leg off with her teeth.

"Oh no!" Olivia quickly hopped off the stepstool and ran outside, panicked. "Declan! What are you doing?"

Her chef glanced over at her, a puzzled look on his face. "What does it look like I'm doing?"

Olivia reached down and scooped up Tater, saving Declan from losing a good pair of chef's whites. "It looks like you're washing that poor dog outside in the middle of winter. Look at her. She's shivering."

Declan rolled his eyes. "It's sixty-five degrees today, Olivia. The dog isn't going to freeze. Would you rather we just handed her over to that high-maintenance starlet with marinara sauce matted in her hair or clean her up first?"

"I'd rather you left it to me." Olivia glared at him,

clutching Tater closer to her chest. "If Priscilla sees this, she's going to go ballistic."

"You're damned right she's going to go ballistic!" barked the fiery redheaded movie star as she stalked out of the kitchen toward Olivia and Declan. "Just what the hell do you think you're doing, manhandling my poor pups?" She pushed Declan out of the way and reached down to pick up the sopping-wet Scooter. The dog wiggled, slipping out of Priscilla's hands and running across the yard, right into a muddy patch where snow had melted just a few days before.

"Scooter!" Priscilla ran after the small shih tzu, and just as she was reaching down to pick her up again, the movie star slipped and fell face first into the mud. "Oomph!"

Declan chuckled.

Olivia ignored him while her heart sank and nausea rolled over her. She quickly ran over to the star and kneeled down, not caring about the mud. "Priscilla? Are you okay?"

The starlet lifted her head and glared at Olivia. "No. I'm not okay."

Swallowing hard, Olivia offered the other woman a hand, but Priscilla ignored it as she pushed herself up and climbed to her feet with her head held high. "I hope you have good insurance, because by the time my lawyers get done with you, you're going to need it."

"Lawyers?" Declan said before Olivia could form any words. "You're kidding, right? Your dogs were left unattended, and when they caused a mess, we tried to help out. And now you're going to sue Olivia for it? Get a grip, lady."

Priscilla's muddy face puckered, and if it were possible

to freeze someone with just their eyes, Declan would've been covered in ice. "My name is not *lady*. You will call me Ms. Cain. And if you ever touch my dogs again, I'll see to it that this inn is shut down and you never work anywhere other than a taco stand. Understood?"

Declan scoffed and took a step forward as if to meet the starlet toe to toe.

Olivia snapped out of her shocked silence and jumped in front of him, facing Priscilla. "Ms. Cain, I am so sorry for this inconvenience. Please, there's no need for lawyers. Send the inn your dry-cleaning bill as well as the grooming bill for your two precious pups. We will be happy to cover them both and anything else that was ruined. If there is anything else we can do to make your stay more comfortable, please let me know and I will personally take care of everything."

Priscilla's demeanor didn't change, but she did give Olivia a curt nod before limping off toward the inn with one dog in her arms and the other one trailing after her.

Once the star disappeared back into the inn, Olivia turned on Declan. "What in the world was that?"

Declan raised both eyebrows as he glanced at the door where Priscilla had disappeared. "I'd say that was an entitled jerk who just threatened both of our careers."

He wasn't wrong, but that didn't mean he hadn't made it worse by antagonizing the woman. Olivia closed her eyes and took a deep breath, trying for some semblance of calm. When she opened them, she met his gaze and in an even tone said, "Your customer service needs work. Do me a favor and instead of antagonizing my guests, how about you just stick to cooking, and I'll deal with any guest relations. Understood?"

Declan snorted his disbelief and shook his head as he walked back toward the kitchen door. He paused just before he slipped inside and glanced back at Olivia. "Whatever you say, boss lady. If you want to let those people walk all over you, that's your business."

"Hey!" Olivia called as he stepped through the door. "That's not—" Her foot slipped out from underneath her, and just like Priscilla Cain had done a few minutes earlier, Olivia went down face-first into the mud. She came up sputtering, "Son of a biscuit!"

Faint laughter sounded from inside the inn, making Olivia's blood boil. She got to her feet, wiped the mud out of her eyes, and with dread weighing down her soul, she walked back into the kitchen, keeping her gaze forward and praying that Declan was busy and didn't see her making a huge fool of herself.

"Nice look, boss," Declan said with a soft chuckle.

Everything inside of Olivia wanted to lash out, to blame this entire fiasco on him. If he'd just let her deal with the dogs, none of this would've happened. Priscilla wouldn't have been insulted, and Olivia wouldn't be covered in mud. A faint voice in the back of her head told her he'd been kind to those dogs and had taken it upon himself to help, despite the fact that they'd run into his kitchen, causing a massive spill that could've hurt someone. But she pushed the thought out of her head. He'd still caused her trouble with Priscilla, and that was a problem that wouldn't go away soon.

Instead of dignifying his comment, Olivia held her tongue, pretending she hadn't heard him, and hurried through the lobby and then into the small apartment behind the registration desk. Once her door was shut, her own small dog came running and then started barking as if she were an intruder.

Olivia sighed. "Apollo, it's me. Hush."

The Lhasa apso stopped barking immediately and tilted his head, staring at her with a confused expression.

"I fell in the mud. Stop looking at me like that." Olivia crossed the room, passed through her bedroom and into the bathroom. The moment she was out of her mud-slicked clothes and was stepping into the shower, a loud cackle echoed off the walls.

Olivia peered into the mirror at the pretty ghost with the glittering eyes and shook her head. "Don't say a word."

"I wasn't going to," Lizzie said.

"Liar."

Her high, tinkling laugh filled the bathroom just before she said, "The chef is trouble."

"You have no idea," Olivia muttered and then ducked underneath the spray of water.

CHAPTER 2

*D*eclan McCabe walked into his sister's kitchen, desperate for a cup of coffee. He'd worked well past midnight, prepping for the coming week to make sure the guests at The Enchanted wouldn't go hungry. The temporary job catering for the movie production wasn't one he'd have ever taken in a million years if it hadn't been for his sister.

And certainly not one working for the gorgeous raven-haired beauty he'd spent one glorious week with six months ago. But when his sister, who happened to be the head chef at The Enchanted, broke her leg, she'd begged him to fill in, and he hadn't been able to say no. Not when his new job at a trendy French bistro in the Napa Valley didn't start until February.

"Tell me you didn't insult Priscilla Cain," Payton asked, her tone full of outrage.

'Okay, I won't,' Declan said, reaching for the jar of coffee beans.

"Declan," she said with an exaggerated sigh. "If you mess this up for Olivia, I could be out of a job. And you know how much I want to stay in Christmas Grove."

He glanced over at his sister as she hobbled into her remodeled chef's kitchen on her crutches. Her blond hair was piled high on her head and her cheeks were rosy with exertion. "Don't you think you're being a little dramatic? Priscilla Cain doesn't have enough power to put your boss out of business."

"No, big brother, I'm not. Olivia told me that if it hadn't been for the producers booking her inn for the next two months, then she would've had to wait for a least a year to open the kitchen. If the main star decides she hates it there and books somewhere else, a lot of them will follow. If she loses their business, I'm out of a job."

"I'm sure she has a contract," Declan said, certain that his sister was just being dramatic. "The studio isn't just going to pull out because of one fussy actress."

"There's a contract, but you know as well as I do that if they pull out, she'd have to sue. Do you really think Olivia has the money to take on a powerful Hollywood studio? She's put everything she has into that inn. She can't afford to have anything go wrong."

Declan turned and stared at his sister. He was still certain she was overreacting, but he did know that she loved Christmas Grove and ever since she'd started working at The Enchanted, she'd become fast friends with Olivia Mann. That friendship was important to his sister. She didn't make friends easily, but when she did, she was loyal to the core. "Are you that worried about losing your job?"

Payton shook her head. "No. Olivia wouldn't let me go unless she absolutely had to. But I am worried that the inn might fail. You know what happened to my job on the coast."

He winced, realizing that he'd forgotten that this wasn't the first time she'd signed on to work at a startup. The restaurant she'd worked at on the coast had gone under in just five months, though it hadn't had anything to do with his sister's stellar cooking skills. It was the owner's inability to manage finances. But it had still been rough.

Payton liked small towns, and had just found her footing in Redwood Bay when the owner had let her go. She'd been devastated when she wasn't able to find another job within thirty miles and had ended up back in the city, which she hated. Now she had a chance to live and work in her favorite mountain town. Losing that chance because her brother couldn't keep his snarky responses to himself would kill him. He wanted his sister to be happy. It was the only reason he'd agreed to work for the woman he'd shared one incredible week with and then never heard from again.

Or at least not until his sister had started working for her.

He still didn't know why Olivia had disappeared and frankly, considering how she refused to acknowledge that they knew what each other looked like naked, he figured he didn't need to know. If she didn't want him, then he damned sure didn't want her.

At least that's what he told himself.

"Declan?" Payton asked, waving her hands to get his attention.

"Yeah?" His gaze flickered to hers.

"There you are." Payton lowered herself into one of the kitchen chairs and added, "Just promise me you won't cause any more trouble for Olivia. She has enough on her plate."

He waved an impatient hand. "It's not like I set out to piss off the actress. It just... happened."

"Yeah, like that week six months ago *just happened*," she said dryly.

Declan bit back a testy reply. He was done talking about that week with his sister. It wasn't any of her business. Besides, that was in the past. There was no need to talk about it. "Do you need me to run any errands for you this morning before I go into work?"

Payton's expression softened as she gave him a half smile. "You really are a good brother, even if you do make my boss crazy."

He had to admit it gave him a certain level of satisfaction knowing that he got under Olivia's skin. The goddess knew she'd gotten under his, though he'd be damned if he ever let that show. "You know I'd do anything for my favorite sister."

"Your only sister," she said with an eyeroll, but there was a genuine smile on her face. He and Payton had always been close, and ever since they'd lost their father a few years ago, they'd been even closer. That's what happened when you only had each other to lean on. "Would you mind stopping by Love Potions and picking up some of Mrs. Pottson's hot chocolate mixes? I'm missing my fix."

"And some caramel kisses?" he asked with a raised eyebrow.

Payton glanced down at her stomach and groaned as she shook her head. "Don't you dare bring those evil things into this house. You know I can't resist."

Declan just laughed. "Sure, sis. I'll make a grocery run, too. If you need anything specific, just text me a list."

An hour later, Declan pulled into a parking spot in front of Love Potions. Downtown Christmas Grove sparkled with twinkling lights and magical snowflakes that didn't melt in the unseasonably warm weather. Across from the shop, a large fifty-foot Christmas tree towered over the town while enchanted snowmen twirled around the nearby skating rink. The entire town took charming to a new level, and Declan understood why his sister loved it so much.

Christmas had always been Payton's favorite time of year. The fact that Christmas Grove embraced the holiday year-round, while also being a small, tightknit community meant Payton had fallen in love with the place instantly. Having grown up in a small mountain town, Payton never had gotten used to big city life. Declan, on the other hand, never wanted to move back to a small town. He preferred the anonymity of the city. It was easier to keep to himself with less chance of busybodies butting into his life.

"Ms. Cain! Ms. Cain!" A woman with a microphone in her hand and a cameraman behind her ran along the cobbled sidewalk toward the movie star who'd just stepped out of Love Potions. "Were you in Love Potions to sign up for *The Great Christmas Grove Cookie Bakeoff*? I know the entire town would just love to watch you when it comes out on the Charmed Network."

Priscilla had started to shake her head, but as soon as the reporter mentioned the Charmed Network, she stopped and stared at the young woman, a calculated expression on her face. "It was picked up by Charmed?"

The young reporter nodded enthusiastically. "The announcement was just made this morning. It'll air as a special on Christmas Eve."

"Well, isn't that exciting for the charming community of Christmas Grove," she said with a bright smile. "How could I possibly say no to a Christmas bakeoff?"

"Does that mean we'll get to see you on our screens this Christmas Eve?"

"Yes, yes it does." Priscilla practically glowed as she told some story about baking cookies with her grandmother every year as a child.

It was obvious to Declan that she'd had no intention to participate in the town event until she'd realized it was an opportunity to get her face on television. Why she suddenly jumped at the chance was a mystery. She was in Christmas Grove because she was starring in a movie. Making an appearance on a baking show was child's play compared to the level of success she'd already achieved. But he supposed she just couldn't pass up the opportunity for more attention.

"What about you, Olivia?" The reporter asked. "I'm sure being featured on *The Great Christmas Grove Cookie Bakeoff* would be excellent exposure for your inn, The Enchanted."

Declan's gaze landed on his boss, who was standing off to the side waiting to get into Love Potions.

She gave the reporter a quick nod. "Yes, yes it would, and since I love baking cookies I can't wait to give it a shot." Olivia glanced in Declan's direction but quickly averted her gaze.

Hmm, what was that about? Declan thought. Did he make her nervous? He smiled to himself, amused that he might be getting under his boss's skin. It was only fair. She got under his often enough.

"Excellent," the reporter said into the camera. "It looks like our town is in for quite the treat, and I'm not talking about the cookies. Tune in Christmas Eve at eight p.m. to celebrate the holiday with *The Great Christmas Grove Cookie Bakeoff.*" She quickly dropped the mic and turned back to Priscilla. "Ms. Cain, I just want to say—"

"Excuse me." Priscilla pushed past the reporter and made a beeline for Olivia.

Frowning to himself, Declan moved in closer, wondering what the dragon lady wanted with his boss now.

The reporter huffed her frustration as she gestured for her cameraman to follow her as she stalked away from the shop.

"I'm going to need you to come up with something spectacular for me to make on that show," Priscilla ordered Olivia.

"Um, what?" Olivia asked, her eyes wide with confusion.

"The bakeoff. If I'm going to go on the Charmed Network, I'm going to need something spectacular. You're going to find it for me, test it out, and then show me how to do it." Her tone had a finality, as if she was certain that Olivia would do whatever she ordered her to do.

"Why would Olivia go through all that trouble for you?" Declan asked, eyeing the woman with contempt. "She doesn't work for you."

Priscilla Cain raised one arched eyebrow and looked down on Declan like he was no better than dog crap on the bottom of her shoe. "If Ms. Mann wants to avoid my negative review of her establishment, then she'll do me this favor." She shifted her gaze to Olivia. "Won't she?"

A muscle in Olivia's jaw ticked just before she let out a terse, "Of course I'll help you with the bakeoff, Ms. Cain. Did you have anything particular in mind, or would you like me to handle all the details?"

"I'd like you to come up with three options. After I sample them, I'll let you know which one I'll be going with." The starlet flicked her hair over one shoulder and then walked off, her heels clacking against the cobblestone sidewalk.

Olivia closed her eyes and let out a frustrated sigh.

"You do realize she'll keep treating you like that until you set boundaries, right?" Declan said, trying to understand why she was letting the star walk all over her.

"It's not a big deal," she said. "It's just cookies."

"You're right. It is just cookies," Declan agreed with a nod. "Until it's not." He squeezed her hand quickly and then strode into Love Potions.

CHAPTER 3

Until it's not. Just who did Declan McCabe think he was? Who was he to imply that Olivia had no spine? She dropped her shopping bags on her counter before reaching down to pick up Apollo.

He snuggled against her chest and licked her cheek excitedly.

Olivia chuckled. "I love you, too, buddy. Now, which one of us is going to tell Declan that neither one of us takes crap from anyone?"

Apollo let out a small bark, indicating he was happy to put Declan in his place. Olivia laughed again and put her dog back down on the floor. "Just for that you deserve an extra treat."

Her dog ran around the counter and promptly sat right next to the treat drawer.

"If only you had the chef trained as well as that dog of yours," Lizzie said, lying sprawled out on Olivia's kitchen table. The hundred-year-old ghost was wearing a flapper dress and had her hair curled and pinned up.

"Are you waiting for a photoshoot?" Olivia asked her. When she'd first moved into the inn, sightings of the ghost had been disconcerting to say the least. It'd been even more unsettling when Lizzie had started to talk to her. But now that Olivia had gotten used to having her around, she actually enjoyed their interactions. Lizzie was warm with just enough sass to keep things interesting.

"Nope. Just waiting for the latest gossip," she said with a wink.

Olivia let out a bark of laughter as she started to put away her groceries. "As if anyone's telling me the gossip. You're the one who has the scoop all the time."

Lizzie's high, tinkling laughter filled the room. "True. When you're a ghost who wanders the halls, you see and hear things." Her expression sobered as she sat up. "Which brings me to why I'm here."

Olivia set down the jar of nut butter and stared at Lizzie. "What did you hear?"

The ghost bit down on her lower lip. "There's a rumor that Leo West is unhappy with his costar and is on the verge of walking out."

"What?" Olivia asked in a hushed whisper. "Leo can't walk. He's the star." Or at least one of them. He and Priscilla were the two principal actors. They'd starred in the television series together and this movie was a sequel. Without Leo, there wouldn't be any movie. "Surely he has a contract."

"He does, but the word is he's so fed up he doesn't care." She gave Olivia a sympathetic look.

"Oh no," Olivia said almost to herself. If Leo walked, that was the end of the movie and every single one of her rooms would be vacant until February. It would be financial ruin. "That can't happen."

"I agree. The question is, what are you going to do about it?" Lizzie got to her feet, and as she walked toward the living room, she vanished just like she always did when she'd spent her energy.

Olivia placed both hands on her counter and hung her head. She'd never regret leaving her disastrous marriage. After years of trying and failing to work out their differences, Olivia had finally left and come home to Christmas Grove with her pitiful divorce settlement. If it hadn't been for an inheritance her mother had left her, she'd never have been able to open the inn. As it was, it'd taken every penny she had to buy and open The Enchanted, and she was grateful to start over. But doing it all by herself, without a partner, was harder than she'd anticipated. She didn't mind hard work. In fact, she thrived on it... usually. Right now, though, she was at a make-it-or-break-it point, and the stress was getting to her.

The bell rang, indicating that someone was waiting at the reception desk. Olivia blew out a long breath, straightened her shoulders, and walked out of her apartment with a positive attitude and her head held high, ready to deal with whatever was waiting for her.

"There you are," Lemon Pepperson said with a bright smile as she handed Olivia some paperwork on a clipboard.

"Your poinsettias are being unloaded from the truck as we speak."

Olivia took the clipboard and glanced out the window at the young man who was wheeling a cart full of the red holiday plants onto the porch. "Thanks, Lemon. I appreciate you sourcing these for me. They're needed for a scene that's scheduled to be shot later tonight."

The set designer had asked if Olivia could arrange for the poinsettias after she'd had trouble sourcing enough of them herself. Olivia had promptly called Lemon, Christmas Grove's Jill-of-all-trades. If there was something someone needed done in town, Lemon was the woman to call. In addition to creating goodwill with the production, Olivia had secured a nice fee that would help her anemic bank account.

"Oh? They're filming tonight?" Lemon asked with a spark of interest in her eyes.

Olivia chuckled. "That's what I hear, but you know how this business is. Things change all the time."

"I bet they do." Lemon peered out the side window and let out a small gasp. "Would you look at that."

Olivia glanced over and spotted Leo West outside, pacing back and forth with his phone pressed to his ear. His face was red, and he looked as if he was ready to blow a gasket.

"Looks like not all is merry with *Merry Me for Christmas*," Lemon said with a snicker.

"I'm sure it isn't anything to do with the movie," Olivia said automatically as she quickly signed the delivery paperwork and handed it back. "Thanks again, Lemon. I'll see you soon, okay?"

"Yeah, soon," Lemon said, still staring at Leo as Olivia guided her toward the front door.

Once Lemon was gone, Olivia texted the set designer to let her know the poinsettias had arrived and then she watched as Leo stuffed his phone into his pocket, sat on a bench in her garden, and then rubbed a hand over his face. He looked exhausted and so unhappy that Olivia just felt she had to do something. Anything to take that frown off his face.

A minute later, Olivia quietly stepped out onto the patio with a wooden tray in her hands. She'd raided the sugar cookies left over from the night before and fixed a couple fresh mugs of coffee.

Leo glanced at her and watched as she placed the tray on the side table next to the bench.

"Cookies might help," she said as she handed him one of the mugs.

"Do you think they'll get a certain actress to take the stick out of her bum?" he asked, nodding his thanks for the coffee.

Startled by his frankness, Olivia let out a bark of laughter. "Honestly?"

He took a sip of the coffee and gestured for her to take the seat beside him before saying, "If it's not honest, I'm not interested in hearing it."

Olivia sat and eyed the conventionally handsome man with his thick dark hair and stormy dark eyes. The man was just as gorgeous in person as he was on screen. But prior to today, she hadn't really interacted with him, and she'd assumed he was just as aloof and self-centered as Priscilla. She couldn't have been more wrong. His gaze was trained on her with interest as if he really cared about what she had to say.

"In that case, no. I don't think cookies are going to change anything when it comes to your costar," she said, giving him a sympathetic look. "The only things I've found that she cares about more than her career opportunities are her dogs. Get on their good side, and you might have a shot."

"Tater and Scooter?" he asked, his eyebrows raised.

"Those would be the ones." Olivia couldn't believe she was having this conversation with Leo West.

"Hmm, I have heard her talk about them like they're her children. You might be onto something," he mused.

Olivia tucked her feet up underneath herself and turned to the man beside her. "Do mind if I ask you something?"

Leo draped his arm over the back of the bench and nodded. "Shoot."

"You might not want to answer," she hedged.

He chuckled. "I've had a lifetime of dealing with the press. Don't worry about me. If I don't want to answer, I'll just say so."

What was she doing? Was she really about to ask this man about his beef with Priscilla Cain? Normally, she would never stick her nose in anyone else's business, but if she could say something, do something to make sure that Leo West didn't walk off this set, then she'd do it. "I might have heard a rumor that you weren't super happy on this set."

He eyed her. "Is there a question in there?"

Olivia chuckled nervously. "No, I guess not."

"What do you want to know, Olivia?"

"You know my name?" she asked, surprised. Everyone except the PA and Priscilla just called her ma'am, which had bruised her pride more than once. No one in their early thirties should ever be called ma'am.

His eyes crinkled at the edges as he chuckled softly. "You introduced yourself when I first got here, remember?"

"Of course, I do," Olivia said, shaking her head. "I introduced myself to everyone, but no one except Tracy the PA, and now you, have actually used my name instead of calling me ma'am. So I'm sorry for my surprise, but do you blame me?"

"No." He shook his head. "Not at all. I guess we're both a little disillusioned with the movie business."

"Are you going to pack up and leave?" Olivia blurted.

Leo blinked at her. "Where did you hear that?"

Swallowing hard, she decided to go ahead and be honest. "Lizzie, the resident ghost. She visits me periodically, and she told me you were talking about leaving the movie."

"Lizzie the ghost?" he asked, sounding surprised. "You have a resident ghost who eavesdrops on your guests?"

"No!" Nausea rolled through Olivia's stomach as she realized that although she'd never asked for Lizzie to spy on her guests, that's exactly what she'd been doing. Had Olivia just made matters worse by opening her big mouth? Surely Leo wouldn't stick around an inn where ghosts were spying on him. She closed her eyes and took a deep breath. "That was… I mean, I never… Lizzie just shows up sometimes. I don't…" Olivia ran a hand over her face. "I'm so sorry. Lizzie was here when I bought the place. I don't have any control over her. She pops up when she wants to. I never intended for anyone to invade your privacy."

Leo let out a loud laugh as he got to his feet and placed his mug back on the tray. "You know what, Olivia? I *was* considering leaving. This entire experience has been hell from day one, thanks to one high-maintenance actress. But it looks like things are about to turn around." He winked at her and then strode toward the inn. Just before he reached the porch, he paused. "Thanks for the info, Olivia. I look forward to meeting you in the garden again sometime."

CHAPTER 4

*D*eclan stared out the window, watching as Olivia cozied up to Leo West. His hand tightened on the clipboard he was holding, making his joints ache. He'd walked out into the reception area to go over the menu for the following week, only to find her sitting with the movie star on the bench, both of their heads together.

What was she doing? Hadn't she told him she wasn't interested in getting involved with anyone who couldn't plant roots? It was one of the first things she'd told him about herself when they'd spent that week together six months ago.

Her words still echoed in his mind. *If I ever get involved again, it'll be with someone loyal. Someone honest. Someone who wants to settle down and plant roots. Someone who will be home with me on Saturday nights.*

No one could tell him that Leo freakin' West was going

to be sticking around Christmas Grove and putting down roots once this movie was made. He was just another version of her ex, someone who was always looking for the limelight. Sure, Leo was a movie star, and her ex, the farmer, had spent all his free time trying to break into the political elite somewhere back in the Midwest or wherever she'd spent the last decade. But it was the same result. Leo couldn't give her what she craved. Normalcy, a true partner, someone who cared more for her than climbing a social or career ladder.

Someone who wasn't Leo, or her ex, or Declan.

Son of a... Declan put the clipboard down on the reception desk and forced himself to turn around and go back into the kitchen. He had no business having an opinion about Olivia's private life. Even if it did make him want to stake a claim. A claim he had no right to. Not when he was moving to the city and had no intention of ever settling down.

Commitment and small-town life were never going to be his thing.

Declan spent the next half hour taking his frustrations out on the vegetables he was chopping up for a hearty stew. He was just turning on the burner to start the stew to simmer when he heard voices in the reception area. After giving the pot a stir, Declan moved into the doorway, watching Olivia and the blond PA as they started dragging in a bunch of poinsettias that had been on the porch.

"The shoot has been delayed," the blond PA said.

"Until later tonight?" Olivia asked.

The PA shook her head. "It's canceled for tonight. Not sure when it's going to be rescheduled. The director thinks there are too many outdoor scenes. He's contemplating renting an indoor space somewhere in town for a holiday party or something." She shrugged. "Who knows?"

Olivia placed a poinsettia on a side table between two wing chairs. "So these are just going to waste?" She waved at the potted plants. "Maybe I can take them to Zach's Christmas tree farm and we can try to resell them." Zach Frost was one of Olivia's oldest friends, and he owned the town's Christmas tree farm. He'd resell the poinsettias in a heartbeat if she asked him to.

"That's a really nice thought," the PA said. "But let's not do that. Production has already paid for them, and I just *know* that as soon as I sold them, the set designer would want to use them for something else."

Olivia nodded. "That sounds about right." She glanced around the reception area. "Gosh, this already looks a thousand times more festive. When do you think it's safe for me to decorate for the holiday? Are there any more scenes scheduled to be shot in here?"

"Let me check." The PA started flipping through a notebook.

Declan had wondered why the inn wasn't decorated for the holiday yet. It was virtually the only place in town that didn't look just like a Christmas card. It made sense that the set designer would want a blank slate when they started working on a scene.

The PA flipped through her schedule book and then

DEANNA CHASE
</>

nodded. "You're in the clear. Go ahead and decorate to your heart's content."

Declan stepped out into the reception area. "Need some help?"

"Oh no," Olivia said, shaking her head. "We're already done here." She turned to the PA. "Thanks for the help, Tracy. Let me know if anything else comes up that I need to know about."

"Will do." The PA slipped out the front door, leaving Declan alone with Olivia.

"I meant with the decorating," Declan said. "Tree, lights, garland?"

Olivia stopped fussing with one of the poinsettias and straightened as she eyed him suspiciously. "You want to help me decorate?"

Declan crossed his arms over his chest defensively. "Yes. Is that so shocking?"

"No... yes." She let out a small huff of laughter and then gave him a wry smile. "I just didn't think Mr. Can't Wait to Get Out of Christmas Grove was interested in anything festive."

"Just goes to show that you don't know me as well as you think you do," Declan said with a smirk. "Now, where do we find these decorations?"

"The tree is outside. Zach delivered it yesterday. And the other stuff is in the attic." She walked over to the front door and poked her head out, pointing off to the left. "How about you get the tree while I go upstairs and get the Christmas boxes?"

"Sure." Declan stood near the reception area as he

28
</>

watched her walk up the stairs. His gaze roamed over her until he found himself gazing at her well-rounded backside. Even while just wearing faded jeans and a T-shirt, she was one of the most beautiful women he'd ever met. He couldn't deny that he'd wanted more than their week together. Much more. Even months later, he was drawn to her in a way that was foreign to him. But he didn't know exactly why. If it had just been looks, he'd have already moved on. This was something more, something he couldn't explain. And it irritated him to no end.

When she got to the first stair landing, she glanced back with a smirk of her own. "Enjoying the show?"

All Declan could do was chuckle. He'd been caught. There was no point in denying it. "Very much so. Feel free to wear those jeans more often."

Her lips twitched with amusement as she shook her head and started climbing the second set of stairs.

Declan waited until her footsteps faded before heading outside to haul in the tree.

Twenty minutes later, Olivia reappeared and said, "It's leaning to the left."

"No it isn't." Declan climbed to his feet and moved to stand next to her. "It's perfect."

"I'm telling you, it's leaning to the left," she insisted as she placed a plastic tote on the floor. "Look at the top of the tree compared to the window. It's…" Her voice trailed off and then she sucked in a small breath. "Did you see that?"

"See what? How it's perfectly lined up?" Declan asked.

She turned to look at him with wide eyes. "Well, it is

now. Didn't you see how it just moved to the right all on its own?"

Was she serious? Declan's brows pinched together as he stared at her in confusion. "I'm not sure I follow. Are you saying the tree magically righted itself?"

"Ah-ha!" Olivia pointed a finger at him. "See. You knew it was leaning. You were just messing with me, weren't you?"

"I don't know what you're talking about." Declan was enjoying this more than he should. He didn't believe that the tree had righted itself on its own, but he sure did love their banter and the fact that the tension between them had eased.

"Fine. Have it your way. The tree didn't move. I must be seeing things," she said with a roll of her eyes.

Declan opened the tote and found a bunch of lights. He pulled them out and walked over to the tree. "How about we just start decorating."

Olivia lifted a box out of the tote. "I still don't know why you're doing this." Her tone was curious as if she really didn't know why he'd be hanging out with her.

"Is it wrong to want to enjoy a little Christmas cheer?" he asked.

She paused for a moment before turning to look up at him. Her lips curved into a pleased smile. "No. Nothing wrong with that at all."

"Good." He winked at her and returned to winding the lights onto her tree. Once he was done, he plugged them in, illuminating the room.

"Ahh, perfect," Olivia said, her eyes twinkling from the

Christmas lights shining in them. "Thanks for your help, Declan. It's always more fun to do this with a friend."

Friend. Is that what they were? Friends? Maybe. But they were more than that. At least that's what his gut was saying. But whatever his feelings, he certainly wasn't interested in discussing them. He gave her a nod. "Yeah, it is. You know what we're missing?"

"Cookies?"

"Yes. And egg nog."

Olivia smirked. "Too bad the only things in my kitchen are cold pizza and beer."

"Do you really have pizza and beer in your fridge?"

"Yep."

Declan pressed a hand over his heart and faked a swoon. "You just might be the woman of my dreams."

She snorted. "You're a simple man, aren't you?"

"Yep. There's absolutely nothing wrong with pizza and beer. In fact, it sounds just about perfect right now."

"No way." Olivia shook her head. "We can't have pizza and beer while decorating my tree. They just aren't festive."

"It's a good thing you have a chef on the premises then." He grinned. "Give me twenty minutes and we'll be in business."

"What?" she said with a laugh. "You can't just happen to have cookies and egg nog in the kitchen."

"I can and I do. I made eggnog earlier, and I have sugar cookie dough already prepared. I was going to make them tomorrow and put them out with lunch. But I can make another batch in the morning."

Olivia's mouth opened in surprise, but she quickly closed it and said, "That would be really lovely."

Declan added one more glass ornament to the tree and then disappeared into the kitchen, acutely aware that he was having more fun with Olivia than he'd had with anyone else in months.

CHAPTER 5

*O*livia sat on a stool in the kitchen, sipping her eggnog as she watched Declan decorate the reindeer- and Santa-shaped Christmas cookies. "You're really impressive, you know that?"

He raised his dark eyes to meet hers. "Did Olivia Mann just give me a compliment?"

"She did." Olivia swirled her eggnog in the glass. "Your decorating skills are next level. Care to teach me some tricks for when I go on that baking show?"

"Oh, I see. You're just trying to butter me up so I'll help you beat Priscilla Cain," he teased.

"Yep. That's exactly it," she said with a definitive nod, feeling a little warm and a lot relaxed from the eggnog. "Anything to get one up on that woman."

Declan laughed. "You're a lightweight, aren't you? That's only your second glass, and I think you're saying things you'd never say if you didn't have a little bit of liquid courage in your system."

"Pfft." Olivia waved a hand, dismissing his comments. "Never mind her. I think I need one of those cookies."

Declan passed her one of the Santas. "It's all yours, but you're going to ruin your cold pizza dinner."

Olivia raised one eyebrow and glanced over at the simmering pot of stew that was still on the stove. "You're not going to feed me?"

"You want some of my stew?" he asked.

"Yes. You've had my stomach growling for the past half hour."

"All right. But only if you help me decorate these cookies first."

"You're on." Olivia moved to sit next to him and grabbed one of the reindeer.

Declan passed her a pastry bag.

"You asked for it." Olivia chuckled to herself as she added the frosting to the cookie, but when her elbow brushed his, all of her amusement fled when a tingle ran up her arm and made her stomach flip. She cleared her throat. "I didn't realize you're left-handed."

"Sorry about that," he said, scooting away to give her room. "I didn't mean to crowd you."

"No... that's not..." She shook her head, frustrated that he'd moved away from her. She knew it was a bad idea to start things up with him again, but she couldn't deny the way he made her feel. Would it be so bad to enjoy herself for a little while? A voice in the back of her head gave her an emphatic *yes*, it would be very bad. She was his boss, and he would never be the type of man she could settle down with. Still, the connection they shared was hard to ignore. "You weren't crowding me."

He gave her a sexy half smile and went back to decorating his cookies.

"Knock, knock," a male voice said from the kitchen doorway.

Olivia glanced up to find Zach Frost standing there with a wreath and a red gift box. "Zach," she said giving him a warm smile. "What brings you by?"

Zach held up the wreath and the box. "We forgot to drop these off when we brought the tree. I was in town, so I figured I'd deliver them." He nodded to Declan. "Hey, man. Nice to see you again."

"Hey, Zach," Declan said.

Olivia glanced between the two of them. "How did you two meet?"

"Declan came by the farm to pick up a tree for his sister," Zach said. "When I learned he was working here, I might have given him some tips on how to best get on your good side."

"Is that why he's baking me cookies and supplying the eggnog?" Olivia asked, only half joking.

"Nope, didn't say anything about your cookie addiction or your love of holiday nog," Zach said.

"So, what did you tell him?" Olivia eyed her friend, wondering if she was going to have to poison him. They'd known each other since they were eight years old, and if there was anyone in Christmas Grove who had the dirt on her, it was Zach.

Zach smirked. "Wouldn't you like to know." He put the box on the counter and leaned the wreath against the door jamb. "Later, Olivia. Declan, give me a call. We'll go get that beer sometime."

Once he was gone, Olivia picked up the box as she turned to Declan. "What did he say about me?"

"That you're a lousy kisser. Something about not enough tongue or too much tongue? I don't recall, but he said you probably needed practice in the kissing department."

"Stop it. He did not," Olivia said with a chuckle. "Zach isn't the kind to kiss and tell."

"Are you sure? He could've been out there telling this story for the past two decades. If that's the case, then dating in Christmas Grove is gonna be really tough for you with that sort of reputation." His eyes crinkled with amusement.

"So you're saying I need to date someone from out of town?" she challenged as she opened the box in her hands.

"No." He reached into the box and pulled out a clump of mistletoe that was tied with a red bow. With a mischievous smile, he hung it over their heads and said, "I'm saying you probably need to start practicing your kissing skills."

Olivia stared up at him. With a quirk of her eyebrow, she asked, "You think you're the one to give me lessons?"

Declan moved in until his lips were an inch from hers. His voice was gravelly when he said, "Don't you?"

Hell yes. Her entire body yearned to feel his lips against hers again. It'd been months since she'd had that one week with Declan, but the echo of his kiss, his touch, his warmth, they all lingered, making her ache for him. She leaned in just a fraction, waiting for him to close the distance.

"Olivia?" he asked, still waiting for her to confirm she wanted this.

"There's mistletoe above us, Declan. What are you waiting for?"

His dark eyes turned molten as he sucked in a sharp breath and then his lips were on hers.

Olivia melted into him, letting herself get lost in the magic of their connection. It had happened before when they were together. She'd never gotten so swept away by anyone before. It was intoxicating and terrifying at the same time. She wanted to give herself over to whatever was between them, but knew she couldn't. Not when he was her employee. Not when he was leaving in a couple months.

Reluctantly, she pressed her palm to his chest and gently pushed him back.

Declan let his lips linger on hers for just a moment before he pulled away. "That was—" he started.

"Because of the mistletoe." Olivia glanced up, and her eyes widened when she saw the sparkling golden light radiating from the bundled foliage. "What is happening?"

Declan followed her gaze. Without saying a word, he carefully set the mistletoe back in the box. The moment Declan let go, the golden light spread from the box to the cookies on the counter. As the light engulfed them, the cookie Santas and reindeer suddenly became animated as they stood up on the counter and whirled around as if they'd been spelled.

Olivia jumped back, holding her hands up. "I'm not doing that."

"You're an air witch, right?" Declan asked her.

"Yes, but you were the one who was holding the mistletoe," Olivia insisted.

"While I was kissing you." He glanced at the dancing cookies and grinned. "It looks to me like these lips of mine might have made you want to dance."

"And it looks to me like your ego is taking up so much space that there's no more room for me." Olivia turned, intending to walk back into the reception area, but Declan caught her hand, stopping her.

"Just one second," he said and pulled her back so that she was pressed against his chest.

"What do you want?"

"This." He dipped his head and gave her another toe-curling kiss.

Olivia told herself she should resist. That she should step back, not let this happen again. But she was too weak. His kisses just melted her brain. Just as she was losing herself in him again, he broke off the kiss, stepped back, and held up the hand that he was still holding.

"This shimmering gold light is coming from you, gorgeous," he said softly. "There's no denying it now."

Olivia stared at their joined hands and felt butterflies flutter in her stomach. Her gaze shifted to his. The amusement that had been there before the second kiss was gone, replaced by something she couldn't quite decipher. Tenderness? Affection? Admiration? She had no idea, but it was far too intense to keep contemplating. She pulled her hand away, watching as the golden light died out. "Air magic doesn't look like that. Not when I use it."

"Is that so?" he asked, sounding skeptical. "Maybe I just bring it out of you."

There was no doubt about that. She cleared her throat. "I need to get back to the reception area so I can finish decorating."

Declan nodded, surprising her when he didn't try to stop her.

"Do you need help?" he asked.

"No, I don't want to keep you from your own work. I've got it from here." She gave him a small smile and headed toward the door. When she glanced back, she noted that the Santas and reindeer had lost their magic and were lying haphazardly on the counter.

"I'll get these plated and bring them out to you in a few minutes," Declan said.

Olivia snorted. "Like I could eat the heads off anything that had just been dancing around your kitchen."

Declan's lips curved into a small smile, that glint back in his dark eyes. "*My* kitchen?"

She hesitated, wondering why she'd said that, but then just shrugged. "For now."

CHAPTER 6

hoa. Declan sat heavily on his stool as Olivia disappeared into the other section of the inn. What had he just gotten himself into? What exactly did he think he was doing, messing around with that mistletoe? There was no denying that he'd been the instigator of that kiss. Sure, Olivia had been just as willing, but he'd started it. He needed to finish it.

He knew he should make Olivia a tray with some stew, walk into the reception area, and apologize for crossing lines both of them knew they shouldn't be crossing.

But the hard truth was, he didn't want to do that. He'd much rather dump everything in the sink and then find Olivia and haul her off to her apartment like he was some sort of caveman. And then keep her there for the next several hours.

His entire body ached to do just that.

Fortunately, he hadn't quite lost his mind yet. Or his

self-control. Forcing himself to put their kisses out of his mind, he finished decorating the rest of the now stationary cookies. Then he cleaned up the mess before turning his attention to the stew. After seasoning it a few more times, he warmed up a couple of homemade rolls and then dished up Olivia's dinner.

With a tray in hand, Declan walked out of the kitchen and into something he could only describe as a magical wonderland. He stopped in his tracks, glancing around the reception area, wondering if his eyes were deceiving him. He knew Olivia was an air witch, but he'd had no idea she was this talented.

Carefully placing the tray on the front desk, he took in the Christmas tree that was adorned with animated red robins, each of them perched on a branch, some of them chirping, while the others had ribbons in their beaks and were turning them into holiday bows over and over again. Tiny angels hanging from the tree were singing softly as their halos glowed in the window along with the twinkling Christmas lights. And that wasn't all. The left front window display had an animated Santa and Mrs. Clause dancing across a pond of ice, while the right window had a set of nutcrackers that had come to life and were dancing the Nutcracker ballet.

Footsteps sounded behind him, and when he turned, he found Olivia standing there with her dog Apollo at her feet. He was wearing plush antlers and looking an awful lot like the dog from *How the Grinch Stole Christmas*. "Olivia," he said. "This is spectacular. You're incredible."

Her face flushed pink as she smiled shyly at him.

"Thanks. I… I'm not exactly sure how I managed such an elaborate display. I cast the spell for the angels and then was thinking about how cool it would be to animate everything else, and then it just happened. It was as if a fairy godmother showed up and waved her wand for Cinderella."

The Lhasa Apso barked once and then ran toward Declan, his teeth bared.

"Apollo, no!" Olivia ordered, but the dog didn't pay any attention to her.

Instead of stepping back, Declan crouched down to the dog's level and pulled out a dog jerky treat. He'd met Apollo before and knew exactly how to tame the beast.

Apollo's snarl vanished as his eyes locked on the dog treat and a second later, he immediately sat, waiting for the snack.

Declan chuckled. "I see he's trained to both attack and sit for his food."

Olivia groaned. "I'm sorry. I don't know what his problem is with tall men. He's fine with everyone else, but when a man taller than me is around, he loses his mind. At least he didn't take a finger off?" she said, making it sound like a question.

"That is a plus, considering I make my living by using my hands." He held the treat out to Apollo, expecting the hellhound to snatch it out of his fingers. But instead, Apollo was polite as could be, gingerly taking the treat before turning around and rushing off to a dog bed behind the counter. He stood and shoved his hands in his pockets. "Was he a rescue?"

"No. The neighbor's dog had puppies, and you know how it goes. As soon as I saw him, it was love at first sight."

"What about your ex?"

Olivia scowled at just the mention of the man. "No. They were never friends. But he didn't discipline Apollo. He never even got near him. I think Paul was afraid of him."

"As he should be if he didn't want to make friends," Declan said with a snort. "Was Paul taller than you?"

"Yep," she said with a shrug. "Only not by much. He hated it when I wore heels. I swear the man had the maturity of a preteen."

Declan knew next to nothing about the man. Olivia hadn't really spoken about him when they'd spent their time together. He'd only heard bits and pieces from his sister. But from what little he did know, he was certain the man was a grade-A jackass. "For the record," he said, eyeing Olivia up and down, "I've never seen anything sexier than those legs of yours when you're wearing heels. If he didn't appreciate that, he's a massive idiot."

Her eyes softened as her cheeks flushed a brighter pink. "Thank you. Paul is an idiot for many reasons. I'll just add that to the list."

Declan leaned against the counter, intensely curious about the man who'd been lucky enough to marry such an interesting and beautiful woman but who'd been stupid enough to lose her. He shoved his hands in his pockets and watched her with interest. "What did you see in Paul? That's his name, right?"

"Yeah." She let out an exaggerated sigh. "Honestly, I have no idea anymore. I guess I was just a naive kid when I met him." She walked over to the desk and waved a hand at the tray. "Thanks for this. You really didn't have to."

"I wanted to," Declan said. "Go on and eat. I know you must be starving. When's the last time you ate anything other than a cookie? Breakfast?"

"Yeah. I think so." She sat down and picked up the spoon. "You're not going to eat with me?"

Declan started to say no. That he still had work to do. But that was a lie. He couldn't do anything more until the stew cooled.

"Come on, Deck. When's the last time *you* ate? You've been here all day. You were in the kitchen before I even left my apartment."

"About ten minutes ago when I decapitated a Santa cookie," he said with a grin.

"Uh-huh. Go get a bowl of stew and keep me company. Apollo's not much for conversation."

How could he say no to that? A few minutes later, he placed his own tray on a small breakfast table on the other side of the reception area and waved Olivia over. "This is more civilized, don't you think?"

She chuckled and then joined him. "You're right. This is more civilized. I suppose I'm just used to eating at my desk."

That work ethic was one of the things Declan admired about Olivia. He'd worked for more than his share of inn and restaurant owners. None of them worked harder than the woman across from him, not only to make her guests happy, but also her employees. In addition to Declan, there was a handful of kitchen staff, room attendants, and a part-time woman who helped Olivia with the front desk. Olivia treated them all with respect, kindness, and most of all gratitude for helping her make her inn as successful as possible.

Well, all of them except Declan. She treated him as more of a nuisance, but even he had to admit that he deserved it. The flirting, and now kissing, mixed in with his pure frustration of wanting her but keeping her at arm's length, made him a royal pain in the backside some days. Who could blame her for being exasperated?

They sat in silence for a few moments while they ate the stew. Declan was about to ask her what she thought of his meal when she suddenly spoke.

"Paul made me feel seen," she said. "I came from this small town where everyone knew me and expected me to take over my dad's restaurant and marry Zach."

"Zach? You dated?" he asked, blinking at her. Why was there a tightness in his gut? Zach Frost was a happily married man. And as far as he knew, she and Zach were just friends. But if they had a past, he knew better than most people how that could tear a marriage apart. He clenched his teeth together, not letting himself go there. Just because his own parents' marriage had been a train wreck, that didn't mean everyone else's would be.

She laughed. "When we were eight. It lasted a week."

Right. He knew that. Zach had told him that, hadn't he? The tension eased from his shoulders, and he tried hard not to analyze why jealousy had suddenly reared its ugly head. *WTF, Declan?* Why had he let himself go there? And over something so ridiculous even. He forced himself to speak in a light tone. "Ahh, your first true love," he teased. "I bet that was hard to get over."

"I think about the time he put a mouse in my bed was when I decided I hated him." She grinned. "Rodents and romance don't mix."

"I can see how that'd be a dealbreaker," Declan said with a chuckle. "It's probably Zach's fault you ended up with Paul. I mean, with an ex that bad, anyone would look decent, right?"

Olivia threw her head back and laughed. "Zach's fault. Oh, I can't wait to tell him that," she said with a humorous gasp. "Just think, all this time I could've been blaming him instead of my poor judgment."

Declan chuckled along with her. And then when he sobered, he caught her eye and asked, "Do you think you'll ever get married again?"

CHAPTER 7

"What?" Olivia asked, completely caught off guard by Declan's question. Marriage? Why was he asking about that? "I... I haven't really thought about it."

"I'm sorry," Declan said quickly, frowning and shaking his head. "I don't know why I just asked you that. It's none of my business."

He was right. It wasn't any of his business. But now that he'd brought it up, Olivia was intensely curious as to why he'd asked at all. They'd already established that he wasn't the settling-down type. They'd talked about it during the week they'd spent together. The week that she'd let herself just enjoy him with no strings attached. She'd told herself that week was her way of really leaving her marriage behind, of letting herself be a little wild and relive the youth that she'd never really had an opportunity to experience. She'd met Paul just one month after heading off to college.

So while all her friends were dating multiple people, going to college parties, and making questionable decisions, she'd been dating Paul and watching from the sidelines.

His question weighed on her mind. Having a family had always been something she'd wanted. Not just a husband, but kids, too. Olivia didn't have any siblings, so her dad was the only family she had left, and he was in and out of her life randomly, depending on what new big adventure he was having. Last she'd heard, he'd opened a bar on the beach somewhere down in the Florida Keys. Sun, bikinis, and rum was her father's motto. It sounded like perpetual spring break to Olivia, and not something she was particularly interested in, so she didn't know most of the details.

After taking a bite of Declan's delicious stew, Olivia looked up at him and nodded. "Yes. If I found the right man, I think I would like to get married again. Why? Are you interested?"

He choked on a sip of water, pounded on his chest, and then cleared his throat. "Um, no, I..." Declan glanced around, looking panicked and as if he'd like the floor to open up and swallow him whole.

She gave the handsome man sitting across from her a smirk. Obviously, she'd known that wasn't where he'd been going with that question; she just couldn't help poking him about it. "Relax. I was just messing with you. But it does beg the question of why you're so averse to the institution. Or is it just the idea of being in a committed relationship that's too hard to fathom?"

Declan took a long sip of his water, keeping his eyes on her. This time he managed to swallow without hacking up a lung. "I just don't understand the concept of legally binding yourself to one person for life. In my experience, even when people clearly love each other, they tend to make each other miserable one way or another. They change, want different things. There's always one who sacrifices what they want for their partner and ends up miserable. I just couldn't do that to someone."

"Is that really what you think marriage is about?" Olivia asked him curiously. "Bending for someone else's dreams?"

"Isn't it?" He raised one eyebrow. "Isn't that what your husband wanted you to do? Live a life he had planned out, despite what you wanted?"

"Yes. And no," she said, frowning as she considered his question. "It's not so much that he expected me to give up what I wanted; it was that he wasn't capable of being the husband I needed him to be, and I didn't see that until it was too late."

"Isn't it the same thing?" he asked, studying her.

"I don't think so." Olivia sat back in her chair. "The vision I had of what our marriage would be was a quiet life on the farm, where we'd raise kids together—"

"And stay in together on Saturday nights?" he asked.

"Yes, but don't make me sound so boring. I like traveling, art, and music. It's not that I wanted to be a homebody." She gave him a sheepish smile. "I just wanted someone I could count on to be present in my life. Someone who appreciated spending quality time with me and, most importantly, thought that marriage and family was a priority, not ambition and always looking for more. It's not that Paul was wrong for wanting something different for his life, it just wasn't the life that I wanted. And I think we were too young to really understand that when we got married."

"I'm not sure stability like that exists," Declan said, his voice void of emotion as if he'd shut down a part of himself.

Olivia reached out and placed her hand over his. "I think it does. Look at Zach and Ilsa, or Holly and Rex, and now Lily and Chase."

He frowned.

"You're skeptical," Olivia said. "Why?"

He shrugged one shoulder as he glanced away. Olivia was certain he wasn't going to answer, making her wonder exactly what had happened in his life that made him so pessimistic about love. But then he turned his gaze back to her and said, "I know they look happy now. And they probably are. Maybe. But you never know what's going on behind closed doors. I'm skeptical it can last. Weren't you and Paul happy at first?"

"I thought so, but looking back on it..." That feeling of utter wrongness washed over her. It was the one she'd felt the day right after she'd married Paul. At the time, she'd brushed it off as nerves. But it was a gut-check type of feeling that she never should have ignored. "If I'm honest, I knew our marriage was a mistake from the beginning. If I'd been more mature and surer of myself, I probably wouldn't have wasted ten years on a man who was never going to love me the way I wanted to be loved. But that doesn't mean I don't believe in marriage. It just means I made some bad choices."

"I just think it's an extremely rare couple who both get what they need from a relationship," Declan said. "More often, one or both end up losing themselves or destroying each other."

Olivia pressed her free hand over her heart. "Damn, Declan, that might be the most cynical view of relationships that I've ever heard. What happened to you?"

"My parents happened," he said, surprising her. She hadn't expected him to answer. Declan pulled his hand out from beneath hers and ran it through his dark hair as he blew out a breath. "They loved each other fiercely. I don't think I ever saw two people who were more in love. They couldn't live without each other, but they weren't happy together either. They were constantly fighting and making up. The public fights were common knowledge. So was the fact that they made up in the backseat of my dad's Cadillac. Do you have any idea what it's like to be a kid with parents like that in a small town?"

That at least partially explained why he'd told her he could never live in a small town. That he was a city guy through and through. It was a fact that small town gossip could be brutal, and she couldn't even imagine what it must have been like for him and his sister growing up with all that gossip. She cleared her throat. "I get it. At least partially."

"You do?" he sounded skeptical.

"Sure." She chuckled softly. "I grew up in a small town, too, you know." Olivia waved a hand toward the window, indicating Christmas Grove. "After my mom died, my dad never stopped to grieve. After the funeral, he never spoke of her again, and instead, partnered with an investor from out of town to start a franchise of his restaurant. Maybe you've heard of it. The Rockin' Reindeer?"

He sounded slightly horrified when he asked, "That place that had its waitstaff dress up like reindeer and sing contemporary Christmas songs year-round?"

"That's the one," Olivia said with a sardonic chuckle. "It wasn't like that when my mother was around. It was just a jukebox kind of diner and a favorite hangout in town. When the dancing reindeer showed up, only tourists frequented the place. Everyone said my dad had lost his mind. That he'd ruined what he and my mom had built. And they were right. The flagship store here in town went under first, then the rest of them limped along until the franchise went bankrupt. He's been chasing his next big idea ever since. He's down in Florida running a bar on the beach."

"That's rough," Declan said. "Do you talk to him often?"

"Only about every six months or so. He calls on my birthday and Christmas." Olivia heard the sadness in her voice and forced a smile. "It's fine. I know where to find him if I need him."

"I guess that explains why you want someone who's happy to stay in on Saturday nights," he said, giving her an easy smile.

"You're probably not wrong."

Declan's expression turned sympathetic. "I'm sorry about your mom. I lost my dad when Payton and I were in high school. My mom never really recovered."

"I'm sorry to hear that." Olivia had the urge to wrap her arms around the man sitting across from her. To hold the teenager he used to be and assure him that everything would be all right. Instead, she gave him what she hoped was a counterpoint to his argument that marriage never worked out. "I think the fact that my dad keeps chasing dreams is a symptom of the fact that he's never gotten over my mom dying. Before her illness, they were happy. Content. Two peas in a pod who loved doing life together, no matter what came at them. I honestly think they'd have made it and would be that older couple in their rocking chairs on the front porch."

He didn't say anything at first, but when Declan finally spoke, he said, "I'm glad you had parents in your life who showed you that a life like that exists." He stood and stacked their dishes. "I still think it's a unicorn situation, but I really hope you find what you're looking for, Olivia. If anyone deserves it, it's you."

Olivia watched as he disappeared into the kitchen, and she felt a pinch in her heart. She told herself it was for him, for the fact that he'd closed his heart off before he found something special. But she knew, deep down, it was because she could fall for him if she let herself. And that would be a disaster of epic proportions.

CHAPTER 8

*D*eclan sat in front of the old boarded-up Rockin'
Reindeer Diner and tried to envision what it
must've been like when Olivia was a kid. The location on a
bluff was stunning with a view of the mountains and the
river.

"It used to be a log cabin with a burned wooden
restaurant sign," Payton said, handing him her phone. "Look
at how charming it was with the wooden reindeer out front.
Looks like the perfect stop after a day on the slopes, right?"

"Definitely." He glanced up at the old metal sign that
hung over the commercialized building that had been
painted to look like something one would find in the north
pole, complete with snowmen columns and a plastic Santa
and reindeer on the roof. "It's a shame what they did to it,
though."

"It looks like something out of an amusement part,"

Payton said, wrinkling her nose. "It's really too bad because the location is fabulous. I could just see an upscale restaurant here if someone wanted to do a major renovation."

Declan glanced at his sister, noting how her eyes were focused on the building. It was as if he could see the wheels turning in her head. They were sitting in his truck, each of them with a sandwich. Payton had wanted to get out and do something, but with her broken leg, about the only thing he could think of was a car picnic. When he'd mentioned it, Payton had jumped on the opportunity to get out of the house. "I'm not wielding any hammers," Declan warned her.

Payton let out a bark of laughter. "Why are you such a stick-in-the-mud? Couldn't you just see turning this place into a fancy farm-to-table restaurant? We'd make a great team."

"Keep dreamin', sis," he said. "No one has that kind of cash. Besides, I have a job waiting for me down in the Napa Valley. Or did you forget about that?"

"No, I didn't forget. Nor did I forget my job with Olivia. But there's nothing wrong with dreaming, is there?" she asked, giving him the look sisters often gave their brothers that indicated they thought he was an idiot.

"That's what I love about you," he said, reaching over and squeezing the back of her neck. "You never let me get away with any of my crap."

"Someone has to keep you in line." Payton took a sip of her water. "Now, tell me why you were so late coming home the other night."

He blinked at her, feeling blind-sided. "What do you mean?"

"What do I mean?" she mimicked in a decidedly irritating tone. "What do you think I mean? You came home after midnight a few nights ago. And since I happen to know the evening shoot was canceled, I'm wondering where you went after work. Did you find a hottie to hook up with? Come on, Deck. Just give me a tiny nugget of information. I need to be entertained before I lose my mind."

"Hottie to hook up with? In Christmas Grove? Who might that be? I swear, everyone who lives here seems to be coupled up already."

"Except Olivia," his sister taunted.

"Olivia and I are just coworkers," he insisted. "You really don't want me messing around with your boss, do you?"

Payton snorted. "It's a little too late for that, isn't it? It's not like you two haven't already seen each other naked."

"Six months ago. And that's over." He started to put the truck in gear, intending to take her back home, when his sister put a hand on his arm, stopping him.

"Do you see that?" Payton pointed toward the trees just beyond the restaurant. "Is that who I think it is?"

Declan peered in the direction she'd indicated, spotting a tall man with dark hair who had a red-headed woman pressed up against a tree as he devoured her mouth. "Good goddess," he muttered. "Is that Leo West and Priscilla Cain?"

"I knew it!" Payton practically shouted. "I'd know that cloud of red hair anywhere. Did you know they were dating?"

"Who says they're dating?" Declan asked, turning his attention away from the couple when Priscilla slipped her hands into the back of his jeans, cupping West's butt. "Looks like it could just be a quick hookup."

"No way. Look at the way they're going at it. There's no chance they haven't done this before," Payton insisted.

"Pay," Declan said with a judgmental shake of his head. "Stop spying on them. It's creepy." Without waiting for a reply, Declan put the truck in gear and quickly pulled out of the parking area.

"I wasn't spying, you know." Payton sniffed. "Is it my fault they just started mauling each other right in front of us?"

"No, but that doesn't mean they needed an audience."

"Maybe that was part of the appeal," Payton said. "You know, some people get off on exhibitionism."

Declan groaned. "Can we stop talking about this now? All of that is TMI. I'd rather not have that image burned on my brain."

"Why not? Two hot people going at it? Who doesn't want to watch that?" Payton pulled the visor down and started peering behind them in the mirror. "I bet they are two of a very small minority of people who actually do look hot while doing the horizontal mambo. The rest of us just look like grunting sea lions."

"Speak for yourself," Declan said.

"Oh?" Payton asked, sounding both amused and interested. "Does this mean you've filmed yourself doing the dirty deed? Was it Olivia? Oh no, don't tell me. If it's her, I really don't need to know that about my boss. Just... blink once if it was Olivia. Twice if it was that hussy you dated in high school your senior year."

Just to mess with her, Declan turned and blinked once.

"Oh, no! Why did you tell me that? Now all I'm going to be thinking about is that video, which, let me tell you, sucks the big one when one of the parties is your brother." She made a face and shuddered. "Scratch that. Tell me lies. Please say it wasn't you and Olivia."

"It wasn't," he said easily, letting her off the hook. "But it would serve you right if I let you keep thinking that. Who asks their brother about a sex tape anyway?"

"Someone who has zero prospects for entertainment. That's who. I have streamed everything there is to stream. I'm down to the shows with subtitles, and you know how I feel about those."

"If you'd wear glasses, you could read them," Declan said, trying to be helpful.

"It's not the subtitles. It's the disconnect from reading and watching. I just feel like it's a lot of work and I miss half the story. Besides, this isn't about that. It's about the fact that I'm bored as hell. You would be too if you had to sit around the house all day and do nothing. No cooking, no Christmas decorating, no ice skating." That last one left her with a sadness echoing in her tone.

Declan reached over and squeezed her fingers. "How about I take you to work today? You can sit propped in a chair and tell me all about how I'm messing up the goat cheese chicken I'm making for the crew tonight."

Payton slapped her hands together and rubbed conspiratorially. "Really? You don't mind?"

"As long as Olivia doesn't care, then I'm fine having a backseat driver in my kitchen. I know when to ignore advice and when it's useful."

"That's questionable." Payton rolled her eyes at him. "You wouldn't know how to take instruction if it bit you in the ass."

Declan laughed. "Guilty as charged. But it's still fun to make you crazy when I don't follow your orders."

"Suggestions," she corrected. "Come on, Deck. I know you don't need me telling you what to do. Your reputation speaks for itself. But it's still fun to debate which goat cheese is better in the lemon chicken, right?"

"Sure," he said, smiling at her as he turned down Main Street.

Payton let out a contented sigh. "I really do love this town. Just look at it, Deck. All the shop windows are animated. The air always smells just a little like burning cedar. And the ice rink near the tree looks divine. If I could walk, I'd be out there twirling with the snowmen as we speak."

"Sounds like a good way to break the other leg." He winked at her. "Remember what happened that year you decided to learn to ice dance?"

"Why are you bringing that up?" she asked, crossing her arms over her chest. "I thought we agreed to never speak of that again."

"You agreed. I didn't." He gave her a predatory grin. "But

don't worry. I won't talk about it until we have an audience. No need to burn a perfectly good story, right?"

"You're evil." She turned to stare out the window while Declan sucked in a breath, pleased with himself for winning that battle of the siblings.

It wasn't long before they pulled into the parking area of The Enchanted. Declan got as close as he could to the front entrance, but it was further than usual as the crew was setting up to start filming. He glanced over at his sister to apologize, but she was grinning ear to ear with a sparkle of interest in her eyes.

"Oh my gosh. Do you think they'd mind if I hung around and watched? This is far more entertaining than staring at you and your chicken."

"Hey, you haven't even seen how I make my chicken yet," he said, pretending to be offended.

"Shut it, brother. We both know your chicken isn't as good as mine. I was just humoring you so I wouldn't have to go back home and watch another rerun of *The Witch Who Spelled Christmas*."

The holiday series had been around for years, and Declan guessed that in a town like Christmas Grove, one could always watch the beloved, light-hearted show that had run for over two decades at Christmas each year. It was a show his sister loved, and if she was tired of it, it meant she really did need to get away from television for a while. "I bet they won't mind. I'll go ask Olivia if we can set you up a chair somewhere out of the way."

"I'll need snacks and plenty of hot chocolate!" Payton called after him.

"Got it." He raised a hand in acknowledgment and kept walking.

The inn was a flurry of activity with lighting crews in the reception area and the kitchen. Declan stopped dead in his tracks when he saw a mic set up over his workstation along with a set of lights. The director was barking orders to the crew around him. When he finally spotted Declan, he said, "This area is off limits, sir. I'm going to have to ask you to leave."

"Where's Olivia Mann?" Declan asked, trying to keep his temper in check. No one had told him the kitchen was going to be used for filming. If that was the case, he was going to have to scramble to figure out how to feed the crew later.

"Who?" the director asked, frowning at him. "I don't know an Olivia."

"The owner of the inn," Declan growled, hating that these people thought they were so important that they didn't even take the time to learn the name of the woman who'd graciously opened her doors to them. Sure, they were paying her, but that didn't mean they had to be A-holes.

"Oh, right." The director glanced around and then shrugged. "She was here earlier, but I don't know where she went."

Declan left without saying a word and entered the reception area, figuring she had to be nearby. She'd want to be available in case they needed anything from her during the shoot. When he didn't immediately spot her, he slipped behind the desk and knocked on her apartment door.

There was no answer as he heard the faint sound of her dog barking from somewhere in the apartment.

"Looking for someone?" Olivia asked from behind him.

Declan turned and spotted the raven-haired beauty. Her face was pinched as she studied him.

Then she swallowed and forced out, "I'm really sorry, but we can't use the kitchen today. The director wants to shoot the next scene in there. It's a new addition, otherwise I would've warned you."

Declan glanced back at the kitchen. "What are these people going to eat if I don't cook?"

"I was thinking we could order take out," she said. "I already told them that if they used the kitchen that we'd need to scramble to find something else for the crew today."

Declan groaned. "That's going to cost you extra. I hope you add it to their bill."

She held up an envelope. "They've already taken care of it. I just need you to find something to serve. Do you think you can handle it? I hate to spring it on you like this, but like I said, I didn't have any notice."

Declan wasn't sure why he was being so surly about the fact the crew was using the kitchen. They had, after all, rented the inn to shoot their movie. Why should that area be off limits? He supposed it was because he'd come to think of the kitchen as his domain. Most chefs were pretty territorial about their space. He just hadn't realized he already felt that way about the inn's kitchen. It wasn't like this was a permanent gig for him. He'd be gone in a few months. "It's fine. I'll run back into town and find some sandwiches or something. But can I ask you a favor?"

"Of course."

"Payton's out in the truck. I was going to take her home, but it turns out that sitting all day every day while a bone heels is nigh-on impossible for her. And although I told her that acting was boring, she seems genuinely excited about the process and wants to stay and watch for a while. Would it be okay to set her up somewhere so that she could watch the filming?"

"Um, yeah. She can hang out with me and the PA," Olivia said, nodding thoughtfully. "We've got a spot behind the cameras in case they need anything."

"She's going to be over the moon about this, Olivia," Declan said. "Thank you."

"No need. I love Payton, and if she needs some help, then that's what I'm here for."

The pair of them made their way back to Declan's truck. Payton was so excited she barely let them help her get over to the inn. She wielded her crutches like an expert, ready to take on the world. Once she was settled into a chair with her leg propped up, Declan left the two women and went in search of some food that he could serve to the crew.

Two hours later, armed with sandwiches and fixings for a large charcuterie board from the local deli, he got to work on setting up a table on the front porch so that the crew could help themselves when they were ready.

Declan was just about to head inside to see how Payton was doing when he felt a hand land on his backside. He stiffened and then spun around, finding Priscilla Cain standing there in just a robe, eyeing him up and down with interest. He quickly took a step back and cleared his throat, forcing himself to remain calm instead of immediately telling her to keep her damned paws off him. If this had been any other situation, he'd have done just that. But he didn't want to cause trouble for Olivia. "Is there something I can help you with?"

Her lips curved into a slow smile. "I can think of a lot of things you can do for me."

"Uh..." Declan glanced around, surprised that they were the only two people outside. When the crew was filming, there always seemed to be a hundred people milling about. "Where is everyone?"

She waved an impatient hand. "It's a small crew today. It's always that way when we're filming intimate scenes."

That explained the robe.

The actress stepped in closer, invading his personal space, and pressed a hand to his chest. "How about when we're done here, you and I find somewhere we can be alone?"

"I don't think that's a good idea," he said automatically as he sidestepped her. "We both have work to do, and I'm pretty sure your costar wouldn't be happy with that development."

Her eyes narrowed, and when she spoke, there was anger in her tone. "What's that supposed to mean? Leo West and I are just colleagues. Why does everyone think that just because people play a couple on television that they must be interested in each other in real life?"

Maybe it's because I saw you locking lips with him earlier?

Declan thought. He could've just said that, but he didn't want her to think that he and Payton had been intentionally following them or something equally as delusional. Instead, he said, "Sorry, my mistake."

The anger disappeared from her eyes as she considered him again. "So, about that alone time."

"Declan's already spoken for," Olivia said, stepping out onto the porch. Her arms were crossed over her chest, and she looked like she wanted to scratch Priscilla's eyes out.

He was? Declan thought. That was news to him.

Priscilla glanced at Olivia and then back at Declan. Recognition dawned in her expression as she waved a hand at both of them. "You two? Doesn't that just figure. The inn owner and her chef. How very cliché. What's next? Will Declan here save Christmas, and you'll be married by New Year's?" There was a mocking in her tone that set Declan on edge.

"We're not—" Olivia started, but Declan cut her off.

"Probably not by New Year's," Declan said. "We haven't known each other that long. But maybe by summer." He walked over and wrapped an arm around Olivia's shoulders, pulling her in so that she was pressed against his side. Then he kissed her temple and squeezed her arm. "The inn would be a perfect place for the wedding, don't you think, babe?" he asked Olivia.

She gaped up at him, making him chuckle.

"I just love it when I catch you off guard." He winked at her.

Olivia finally seemed to catch on that he was just putting

on a show for Priscilla. It was her fault after all. She was the one who'd said he was already taken.

"I think a Christmas wedding might be better," she said, gazing up at him with adoration. "All the snow and twinkle lights. It would be magical. Don't you think?"

The image of her in a white dress with holly berries tucked into her hair was so vivid in his mind that it almost seemed like a vision. And for once, he wasn't sure he hated the idea.

Priscilla let out a huff of irritation. "I should've known you were way too small town for me." She glared at Declan for just a moment before stalking back into the inn.

Olivia immediately stepped out of Declan's embrace and placed her hands on her hips. "Why did you tell her that?"

He shrugged. "Why not? You're the one who told her I was taken. Who else was going to be my stand-in girlfriend?"

"I don't know. Maybe one who was away on business? Or visiting family overseas for the holiday? But not me. Now we're going to have to pretend to be together while they're here."

Declan narrowed his eyes at her. "Are you mad at me?"

She huffed. "What gave it away?"

He chuckled as he shook his head. "Why did you tell her I wasn't available anyway? I could've just said no."

"I was trying to save you from her harassing you for weeks. Priscilla Cain isn't a woman who takes kindly to the word *no*. You're welcome, by the way."

"Thank you," he said, enjoying this more than he should.

"So, about date night. How about a sleigh ride through town?"

"Date night?" she asked, looking dumbfounded. "You do realize we aren't actually dating, right?"

"On the contrary. It looks like we are, at least until the film wraps. Friday night? Seven? I'll pick you up then." He grinned at her and then disappeared into the inn to check on his sister.

CHAPTER 9

What have I gotten myself into? Olivia stared into her bathroom mirror, wondering why she'd gotten dressed up for the fake date with Declan. It'd been three days since he'd told Priscilla that the two of them were dating. Since then, the actress had been shooting her daggers every time she looked at Olivia. But at least Priscilla hadn't hit on Declan again.

So mission accomplished, right?

Except now Declan was kissing her hello and goodbye on the cheek every day when either Leo or Priscilla were around. He'd even held her hand one afternoon when Leo had asked for suggestions on where he could get some winter gear in town. It seemed he hadn't packed enough clothes for the freezing temps that had started a couple days ago.

After Leo had left, Olivia had shrugged Declan off and told him he was going too far, but it hadn't deterred him.

He'd shrugged and said, "I'm just following your lead, Olivia."

He was infuriating.

But she couldn't keep lying to herself. The fact was that she liked the attention. Declan was easygoing and fun and, in his own way, attentive. He always seemed to show up with food or hot chocolate when she was running on fumes. Like that morning after she'd taken Apollo for a walk, as soon as she walked in, he had hot chocolate and warm homemade croissants waiting for her at her desk. They weren't on the craft services table, nor were they left over from breakfast. He'd just taken the small batch out of the oven and was saving the rest of the dough for later.

How was she supposed to keep a man at arm's length when he was making her fresh pastries? He wasn't playing fair.

Now she was going on a date with him. A sleigh ride through town. Just the two of them. She should call it off. There was no reason to go through with it. Not with the way Declan had been acting ever since they'd lied and told Priscilla they were dating. No one questioned the lie. Not even Payton, who'd already mentioned that she thought Declan and Olivia were perfect for each other. When Olivia told her it wasn't like that, she'd waved a dismissive hand and said, "That's what Declan said, but I've got eyes. It's clear you two are into each other. Just be careful, okay? I don't want you to be hurt when he leaves."

Well sure. They had spent an incredible week together six months ago. But that still didn't change the fact that they wanted different things out of life. Dating Declan was a nonstarter. She would not put herself in a position of sacrificing her own needs for someone else. She'd learned that lesson the hard way.

"He's into you." Lizzie's image appeared in the mirror, watching Olivia carefully.

"No he isn't. Not really," Olivia insisted. "He's just playing around. After Payton is healed, he'll be gone and that will be the end of that."

"I mean Leo West. He watches you when he thinks you're not looking."

"Leo West?" Olivia let out a huff of disbelief. "We had one conversation out in the garden. There is no way a movie star is interested in me."

"Maybe he's just interested in getting you into bed." Lizzie pumped her eyebrows. "That would be some notch on your bedpost."

"I'm not looking for that." The idea of having some short-lived affair with Leo West was ridiculous. Olivia had never been the type to get starstruck by a celebrity. For her, attraction was about a deeper connection. It wasn't just physical. And while she liked Leo well enough, the spark just wasn't there.

Not like it was with Declan.

The night she'd sat down next to him at the bar in a tapas restaurant in San Francisco, they'd connected over the delicious polenta and short ribs and the goat cheese crepes. They'd spent the night talking about food and had ended up making plans to eat again the next night at a Michelin star restaurant. She was so drawn to him and so comfortable that it hadn't taken long before she'd invited him back to her hotel room. It was the first time in her life that she'd thrown caution to the wind and shared her bed with someone before she'd dated them for at least several weeks.

"I'm just saying that maybe the best way to get over that chef, is to get under the sexy movie star," Lizzie said just before she vanished into thin air.

"No." Olivia stared into the mirror at herself, taking in her fierce expression and her bright determined eyes. "It's never that easy." If it were, she wouldn't be thinking about Declan every night when she climbed into bed by herself. The last thing she needed was to complicate her life with a movie star who would leave in two months and never look back.

Apollo's nails tapped on her tiled floor as he moved to stand next to her.

Olivia reached down to pick up her dog and held him against her chest as she scratched his ear. "You're the only love I need in my life, right, buddy?"

He responded by licking her cheek.

She grinned at him. "I love you, too."

Still holding her dog, she made her way to her small kitchen where she set Apollo back on the floor. He promptly sat at her feet and looked up at her with adoring eyes. After fetching him a treat, she petted him one last time, grabbed her purse, and then went to meet her date.

Declan was standing next to the Christmas tree, his palm open. One of the robins from the tree had hopped onto his palm and was tweeting away in a tune that sounded a lot like "Jingle Bells."

Olivia grinned at him. "How did you make that happen?"

"I have no idea," he said, his expression full of wonder. "I was just standing here when the robin pecked on my finger. Once I opened my hand, it fluttered onto my palm and started to sing."

Shaking her head in wonder, Olivia said, "I don't think I'm ever going to get used to this place."

"The inn?" he asked, sounding surprised.

"Yes, the inn, but what I really meant was the magic that seems to be concentrated here. I didn't spell those robins to do anything like that. My air magic isn't going to make them sing."

"Really?"

"Nope." Olivia put her hand out and smiled as one of the robins hopped onto her hand. "Making inanimate objects sing isn't in my repertoire. I have to assume it comes from the magic inherent to the inn itself."

"It sounds like you got yourself a real special place." Declan held his hand up to the tree and waited patiently until the robin moved back onto a branch. Then he turned to Olivia and grabbed her free hand. Tracing his thumb over her knuckles, he asked, "Are you ready for me to show you Christmas Grove?"

Olivia eyed him with a mixture of amusement and confusion. "You do remember that I grew up here, right? Shouldn't I be the one who's showing you the town?"

"Nope. Tonight you're going to see your town through the eyes of a newcomer."

"Why?" she asked.

"Because, Olivia, sometimes seeing a place you love

through a new lens makes you fall in love just a little bit more. And that's what I want to give you tonight."

Olivia blinked up at him, slightly confused. She wasn't sure why he thought she needed to see Christmas Grove through new eyes, but she was intensely curious to find out what he had in mind. "Okay then. Show me your version of my town."

"Gladly." He held his arm out to her.

Olivia slipped her arm through his and let him lead her out into the night.

"So, where are you taking me first?" Olivia asked once they were in his truck.

His lips twitched into a small smile. "That's a surprise."

"It can't be that much of a surprise since you're headed into downtown. There just aren't that many places to go."

He laughed. "You're not wrong about that. But I'd still rather you be surprised."

"All right," she said with an exaggerated sigh. "I guess I'll just have to find a way to entertain myself until we get there." She reached over and turned on the radio. After finding Christmas Grove's one and only radio station, she sat back and sang along with Wham's "Last Christmas."

Declan glanced over at her and smirked. "When's the last time you listened to this station?"

"Huh? Why?" she asked.

"Just wondering. It's not what you play at the inn when you have music playing."

"You're right, it's not. I usually prefer something less pop, softer and more mellow for the inn. But when I'm in the car? I usually listen to something that makes me want to dance."

"If I were to get in your car right now, would this station come on the radio?" he asked.

"Nope. I think I have it set to a top forties pop station." She let out a laugh. "Why are you so interested in my music preferences?"

His eyes gleamed with mischief when he glanced over at her. "Just pointing out that you're already stepping outside of your routine."

"By listening to Christmas music?" she asked. "I think you're reaching, buddy."

"Maybe so," he agreed as they drove down Main Street and then turned onto a dirt road.

"Is this a situation where the charming guy takes the girl out and then she is never heard from again?" Olivia asked him as she peered into the darkness. She couldn't ever remember being out on this road and had no idea where Declan was taking her.

"Do you really think I'd do that to my sister?" he teased. "If you went missing, she'd be out of a job."

"Oh, I see. It's not so much that you're not a creeper, it's that you love your sister more?" she asked, barely able to contain her laugh.

"Something like that." He reached over and squeezed her hand just as he pulled into a small clearing that overlooked the river.

Olivia peered out the windshield at the full moon that was shining down over the serene river. Peace settled over her, and she wondered why she'd never known this bluff existed. Without saying a word, she slipped out of the truck and moved over to the edge, letting the woods, moonlight, and water soothe her soul.

"It's just lovely, Declan," she whispered, not wanting to disturb the peacefulness of the moment.

"I found it a week after I got into town. It's where I come when I just need to decompress."

"I can see why," Olivia said, turning to him. "It's... magic."

"You're magic," he said softly as he raised a hand and cupped her cheek.

"Declan, I..." What could she say? That they weren't really on a date? That Declan shouldn't be acting as if they were anything more than just friends? But how could she say that when they were standing on a bluff with the moonlight shining down on them and all she wanted to do was push up on her toes and kiss him.

"Shh." He brushed his thumb over her cheek, and just when she thought he'd lean in to give her the kiss she desperately wanted, he let his hand drop and turned away to study the river. "It's time to make a wish."

"What?" she asked, taken off guard.

"A wish. It's a full moon." He squeezed her hand before stepping forward and lifting his face toward the light.

Olivia watched him, her heart suddenly beating faster as she studied the serene expression on his handsome face. The man was beautiful both inside and out. And it hit her suddenly and with such force that she almost took a step back. This man was special. He was more than any other man she'd known. He touched her soul in a way that no one else ever had.

"Did you make your wish?" Declan asked without looking at her.

"I think so," she said quietly and turned into the moonlight so that her heart would settle. So that the instinct to wrap her arms around him would pass and she could go back to pretending that she wouldn't be crushed when he left Christmas Grove.

CHAPTER 10

This was a mistake. The words echoed in Declan's head over and over as he parked his truck near the pickup spot for the horseless carriages that took people around to look at the holiday lights of Christmas Grove.

When Declan had planned the date, he'd meant for it to just be a fun night out on the town. The idea was meant to both make it clear to Priscilla that he was taken and not interested in dating her while also enjoying an evening with Olivia as friends. But when they'd been at the bluff over the river, something had shifted. This was no longer just a pair of friends out for the evening. He was falling for her. There was no denying it. Declan wanted her.

But he knew there was nothing he could do about it. Not when he knew she needed someone who would stick around, who wanted to grow old on her porch. He wasn't that man, and he wanted her to get everything she deserved.

In the meantime, he was going to do everything in his

power to make sure she had a great night, one that she'd always remember so that when another Paul came along, she wouldn't feel tempted to go down that path again.

"Do you really think I've never done the horseless carriage ride tour before?" Olivia asked, giving him a look of disbelief.

"Not like this one," he said as he climbed out of the truck and hurried around to her side to help her out.

"Does this mean our carriage is going to fly like Santa's sleigh or something?" she asked.

He chuckled. "Now that would be memorable, wouldn't it?"

"Is that a no? Because if it is, I'm going to be really disappointed."

"Oof." Declan pressed a hand over his eyes. When he dropped it, he added, "I guess I've failed at the date. Do you mind humoring me anyway?"

"I guess. I mean, we're here already." She spun around and then headed for the carriage that was waiting for them.

"That's the spirit." Declan helped her into the carriage and then climbed in after her. Once they were settled, he said, "Take us to the mountain."

Olivia gave him a curious look. "The mountain?"

"You'll see." Declan wrapped an arm around her shoulders, pulling her in for a sideways hug.

Olivia went willingly and pressed her head against his chest. When she didn't pull away, he relaxed into the seat and started to caress her gorgeous raven-colored hair.

The carriage rolled past the large estates on the north end of town. Each of them had elaborate light displays with animated reindeer, penguins, elves, gnomes, and snowmen. Every house seemed to be more impressive than the last. Declan hadn't seen anything like it before, but it was clear that Olivia had. She put on a running commentary of how each house had changed over the years. It wasn't until they made a turn down a dark, tree-lined street when Olivia stopped with her history lesson.

"Another dark, lonely road?" she asked. "Let me guess. This time it's a cemetery?"

Declan laughed. "It's Christmas season, not Halloween."

"So Santa's workshop then? I wouldn't mind seeing it, but if I'm pressed into service and forced to make a thousand yo-yos before I'm liberated, I'm going to be pretty upset and your Yelp review is going to be terrible."

"Not Santa's workshop either, thank goodness. Because you know I live in fear of having a bad date rating on Yelp."

"You should," Olivia said with a giggle. "If anyone googles you, they'd learn all about how you didn't feed me before you gave me up to Santa and his elves."

"Didn't feed you?" he asked as the carriage came to a stop. "Are you sure about that?"

Olivia glanced past him at the small cabin that was lit up with twinkle lights. The door opened, and a woman dressed in black pants and a red sweater appeared holding a couple of menus.

"Welcome to The Mountain. Declan and Olivia?" she asked.

"That's us," Declan said as he jumped down from the carriage. He held a hand out to Olivia who took it and climbed down after him. He squeezed her hand. "I hope you're hungry, because the chef has prepared something special for us tonight."

Olivia gaped at him. "How did you do this?"

Declan grinned at her. He'd hoped that she'd remembered the restaurant they'd had dinner at down in in Half Moon Bay during the time they spent together in San Francisco six months ago. It looked just like the cabin in front of them, but it had been called The Hills. "Let's just say that the chef owed me a favor."

"You're incredible, you know that, right?" she said with a look of wonder. "How did you even find this place?"

"My sister was looking at a house down this road. I saw it the day we came to look at it. It turns out the owners rent it out, so here we are." He tugged her toward the house.

Moments later, they were seated by a large picture window that had a view of the entire town of Christmas Grove. The Christmas tree on Main Street was lit up in the distance, illuminating the snow-capped buildings and trees. Everything sparkled, turning Christmas Grove into something that resembled a jeweled wonderland.

"This is..." Olivia turned her attention to the sights outside the window, her eyes wide with wonder. "I can't believe how beautiful and incredible this is," she said. "Thank you, Declan. It's perfect."

"Wait until you taste the food before sending in that rating," he warned with an easy smile. There was no way she wouldn't be blown away by the private dinner the chef had already prepared.

"It's going to be a solid five stars," Olivia said. "You can count on it."

It wasn't long before their wine glasses were filled and the food started to appear. As promised, each bite was even more delectable than the one before. Olivia seemed to have trouble forming words, instead opting for moans of pleasure that made Declan ache for the beauty sitting across from him.

"If you keep that up, this platonic date is going to turn into something decidedly X-rated," he told her, keeping his tone light and playful.

"You wish, McCabe. The only issue we're going to have is that I might take my clothes off and roll around in this sauce. I swear, I've never tasted anything so mouthwatering in my life."

The image of her stripping down to roll around in the lemon butter sauce was almost too much for him to bear. He glanced away from her and cleared his throat. "That's quite a visual."

Olivia giggled, and he noticed the rosy flush on her cheeks. She'd only had a glass and a half of wine, yet she was tipsy. Maybe even a little bit drunk. Goddess, she was gorgeous with that flush and the sparkle in her eyes. Though now that he knew she was intoxicated, that meant he couldn't even contemplate taking her home when the date was over. Not that he'd had that in his plan for the evening. They weren't really dating, after all. But still, he had to admit that there was some small part of him that hoped they'd find their way back together even if it was only for one night. But not when she was drunk. He wouldn't go there.

Olivia continued to talk about how much she liked the

food, prompting Declan to call for the chef. When he arrived, thick French accent and all, Olivia put her fork down and gushed about how fantastic it all was. The chef puffed up his chest as he swelled with pride.

When Olivia was done offering him her first born for a few of his recipes, he said his goodnights, told Declan he was a lucky man, and then left, leaving his crew behind to clean up and to tend to any other needs.

Olivia had one more glass of wine before Declan swept her out of the makeshift restaurant so that they could continue their date.

"There's more?" Olivia asked once she was settled back in the horseless carriage as it took off down the tree-lined street back toward town.

"There's more," Declan said and reached for her hand.

"We're not supposed to be doing this," Olivia said, holding their entwined fingers up.

"Says who?" he asked.

"Me. That's who," Olivia said, sounding irritated. "We're supposed to be friends. This is a fake date. Holding hands is off limits."

"Okay." Declan immediately let go of her hand. "How do you feel about me holding you as I twirl you around the skating rink?"

"That's fine, except you never said anything about skating," she insisted. "That's a pretty standard activity around here in the month of December. I thought this date was about seeing the town through your eyes?"

"It is. I can't wait to show you what I see when I'm spinning around on ice," he said with a confident smile.

"In that case, neither can I," she said, closing her eyes as she leaned into him.

Declan pulled her in close, reveling in her warmth, and he was disappointed when the carriage came to a stop at the town square. If he'd had his way, he'd have never let go of the lovely woman who'd spent the evening teasing him and enjoying every moment he'd planned.

"Ohh, look at that," she said. "We have the entire rink to ourselves tonight," Olivia said as she jumped out of the carriage and this time held her hand out to him. "Come on, McCabe. Show me your moves."

Goddess, she was adorable. "You're on, Mann. Let's go put our skates on so that I can wow you with my skating expertise."

The way she laughed told him she had zero confidence in his ice-skating skills. He didn't care, because in just a few minutes, he was going to prove her very wrong.

Once they had their skates on, Declan walked onto the ice and gestured for Olivia to join him. When she hesitated, he asked, "Are you okay?"

"Yeah. Fine. I just... the last time I was on the ice, I fell and broke my tailbone. I'm not eager to repeat the experience."

"Have you ever heard of the concept of transferring your magic to another person?" Declan asked her.

She frowned and shook her head. "No. What does that mean? That someone can steal someone else's power?"

"No. Not exactly." Declan skated in a circle while he tried to figure out the best way to explain his magic without making it sound like he was some sort of magic thief. "It's when one witch can give another their power so that the other person can borrow it for a while. I want to try that with the ice skating."

"You want to give me your power so that I can ice skate?" she asked, sounding incredulous.

"Yes. Exactly." He gestured for her to join him on the ice. "Did I ever tell you that I used to be a pretty good ice skater?"

Olivia, who was slowly making her way toward him, shook her head. "No. The subject never came up."

"I'm not surprised. That was a time I generally like to forget. Everything except for the ice skating. I was pretty good. Almost made it onto the national team, but missed out due to an injury."

"That's terrible," Olivia said, biting her bottom lip as she struggled to keep her feet underneath her. "But what does that have to do with sharing your power?"

"This." Declan held his hands out to her, and the moment he did, he felt his magic zap into her. Her legs immediately stopped shaking as she stood up taller and glanced around with a smile on her face.

"Wow," she said. "It feels as if I grew up on the ice."

"You haven't seen anything yet," Declan said. And then with his hands clutching hers, he took off, pulling her with him as the pair flew across the ice.

Olivia let out a cry of excitement, and kept pace with him for the next thirty minutes as they did turns, complicated blade work, and even a couple of jumps. Olivia kept up with it all, matching him trick for trick, stride for stride, and when they landed the last jump, she threw her head back and raised her arms in the air as she said, "This is the best damned date I've ever had. Thank you, Declan McCabe. I don't know how I'll ever be able to return the favor."

"You already have," he said, tugging her back to him and initiating one last twirl before he took her home for the evening.

Sitting outside her inn, Declan didn't dare shut off his truck. If he got out, the chances of him leaving before morning were next to zero.

"Did you have a good date?" he asked.

"The best," she said softly from her place in the shadows on the other side of the truck. "I honestly have no idea how a mere mortal will ever be able to compete with that."

"Then my mission is complete." Declan leaned across the cab, kissed her on her cheek and then pushed her door open, willing her to get out and disappear into her inn.

"I guess that's my cue," she said and slipped from the truck. Just before she closed the door, she said, "Good night, Declan. Sweet dreams."

He watched her walk slowly up to her front door. Once she was there, she paused and glanced back at him.

Just go inside, Olivia, he silently begged her. *Just go inside.*

He let out a sigh of relief when she finally unlocked her door and went inside. It took all his willpower to not follow her. Instead, he put his truck in gear and drove across town to his sister's house.

He'd just walked in and shut the door behind him when he heard his sister say, "You're just asking for trouble, Declan. You know this won't end well, right?"

"It wasn't a real date," he said.

Payton snorted. "The hell it wasn't. That look on your face tells a very different story."

"There's no look. I'm just tired," he insisted as he passed her and strode into the hall toward the room he was staying in.

"You just keep telling yourself that, brother. But we both know that if you keep this up, you'll both be heartbroken when it's time for you to leave."

Declan slipped into his room and slammed the door behind him. Slumping back against the door, he ran both hands through his hair and pulled at the ends. Because dammit, Payton was right. He'd meant for the night to be fun. Instead, it'd been *incredible*, and Declan knew he'd already started to fall in love with Olivia.

What the hell was he going to do about that when it was time to leave for his job in Napa? That was the million-dollar question.

CHAPTER 11

*O*livia smiled to herself as she felt the warm weight of Declan cuddled in beside her. The one thing she'd missed since she'd become single was feeling that weight of someone next to her in the bed, having someone wrap their arm around her, making her feel safe while she slept.

Not that she wanted to do anything remotely resembling sleep. Not when she had a hot man in her bed. She rolled over and was just about to reach for Declan when she felt a wet tongue lap at her face.

Her eyes flew open as she let out a cry of surprise only to find that her bedmate wasn't Declan at all. It was Apollo and he was standing over her, his tail wagging as he went in to give her another round of morning kisses.

"Apollo!" she laughed as she turned her face, letting him lick her cheek before she scooped him into her arms and gave him a snuggle. "You rascal. You interrupted a very nice dream."

He let out a bark and jumped off the bed, his tail wagging as he waited for her to follow suit.

"You're relentless," she said with a sigh and climbed out of bed. Her dog followed her into the bathroom while she completed her morning routine and then the moment she stepped out of the bedroom, he ran over to his dog dish and sat, just waiting for his breakfast.

Once he had his kibble and fresh water, Olivia got herself a cup of coffee and then followed Apollo to the back door where she let him out into the backyard that was covered in a fresh layer of snow.

Olivia loved this part of the morning. The sun had just come up, and the day was full of so many fresh possibilities. She took a sip of her coffee and filled her lungs with the cool mountain air. The snow would mean there were additional chores to handle, but it was worth it to be able to enjoy the beauty of the season.

Once Apollo was done doing his business, he ran back inside to Olivia where she quickly scooped him up so that he wouldn't track his wet paws all over her floor. Once he'd been toweled off, she released him and went to make her breakfast.

Before she could get to the toaster, there was a loud knock on her door.

Olivia glanced down at her robe and fuzzy slippers and groaned. There were definitely disadvantages to living on the premises. It meant she was never truly off work.

Bang, bang, bang!

"I'm coming. Hold onto your shorts," she called as she clutched her robe tighter around her and went for the door, finding Tracy, the PA, standing there, panic on her white face. "What's wrong?"

"It's Priscilla's dogs," Tracy said in a hushed whisper. "They got out again, and she's losing it. She said a ghost did it and if anything has happened to them, she's going to sue."

"She thinks a ghost—" Olivia shut her mouth mid-thought and shook her head. There was at least one ghost who lived at the inn. But would Lizzie ever do anything to put Priscilla's dogs in harm's way? Olivia didn't think so. She was always kind to Apollo. But that didn't mean Lizzie hadn't gotten irritated by the likes of Priscilla Cain. That woman could put anyone on edge. "Never mind. Let me throw some clothes on, and I'll be right out."

"Hurry," Tracy said as Olivia shut the door in her face.

After pulling on a long-sleeved thermal shirt and the first pair of jeans she could find, Olivia stuffed her feet into her tennis shoes, grabbed a sweatshirt, and hurried out into the lobby.

The inn was pure chaos. Tracy was pacing right in front of Olivia's door. The production crew was busy setting up for another day of filming. And she heard the sound of dogs barking so incessantly that Olivia was sure a pack of squirrels was tormenting them.

"There you are," Priscilla's angry voice called from the other side of the room.

Olivia turned and spotted the actress. She was dressed to the nines in a sparkling black ball gown, six-inch stiletto heels, and she had a diamond tiara atop her red curls.

Everything about her screamed royalty except for the angry scowl on her painted face.

"Do you see what's happening out there?" She pointed out the picture window at her dogs. They were running around under a tree, each of them caked with dirty snow while they chased a pure white cat who was leaping from limb to limb and swatting them each time they got close to her.

Okay, not squirrels. The tormentor was a vindictive cat.

"I do see. Why are Tater and Scooter outside?" Olivia asked, just to see if the actress would voice her suspicions about the ghost.

"Someone at this inn let them out. They were in my room while I was down in wardrobe getting ready for this morning's shoot. If you don't get to the bottom of this and get them rounded up and cleaned up immediately, I'll make sure no one ever sets foot in this place again. Do you understand?"

The urge to sigh at Priscilla's hysterics was strong. But Olivia kept her reaction in check and just said, "Of course, Ms. Cain. I'll do everything I can to remedy this situation."

"You bet your ass you will," Priscilla called after her as Olivia slipped out the front door.

Olivia wondered what it must be like to go through life feeling so hostile all the time. It couldn't be good for the woman's blood pressure. And it likely aged her faster. It wasn't as if the dogs were playing in the street. They were in a closed-in garden area on the side of the inn. The only danger right now was the cat that looked like it was ready to swipe a nose off.

"Tater, Scooter," Olivia called from the other side of the gate. "Come here."

The two shih tzus immediately gave up on the cat and ran over to the gate, both of them jumping up and down excitedly to greet her.

"Well, you two certainly have made a mess of yourselves, haven't you? Your mom is beside herself. You know that, right?"

Both dogs wagged their tails and pawed at the gate, wanting her attention.

"Okay. How about this. I'll get your leashes and the dog crate and then all three of us will make a trip to town to get you all glammed up. How does that sound?"

"Looks like you could use some help," a man said from behind her.

Olivia turned and spotted Leo West coming toward her with two leashes. When he reached her side, he handed one to her and then reached down and secured the other one to Scooter's collar. "Thanks," she said as she clipped Tater into the leash. "This isn't exactly how I planned to spend my morning, but hanging out with two cuties isn't exactly a hardship."

Leo looked her up and down and grinned. "What *were* you planning to do? Enter a mud wrestling contest?"

"Huh?" Olivia glanced down at herself and muttered a curse when she realized she was wearing jeans with muddy dog prints on them. Apollo must've gotten to them one night before she'd wiped his paws. "No. I was planning on working on my advertising budget for next year, but that was thwarted by these two cuties." She waved at the messy dogs. "But I guess I dressed perfectly for the occasion without even realizing it."

He chuckled and opened the gate to let the dogs out.

Olivia handed him the leash she was holding. "Can you keep an eye on them while I grab my crate? Gotta get these two into town and get them groomed before their mother has a brain aneurysm."

"Not a problem." Tater and Scooter went with him willingly, and when he crouched down to give them attention, they immediately love-bombed him with kisses.

Olivia wondered how it was possible that Priscilla, the woman she was quickly starting to mentally refer to as the ice queen, had ended up with two giant furry sweethearts. After finding her traveling crate, Olivia hurried out to her Subaru Outback and gestured for Leo to join her with the dogs.

"Wanna help me get these trouble makers situated?" Olivia asked him. "Or are you needed for the shoot this morning?"

"Nope, no call sheet for me," he said with a grin. "They cut my part in the scene, so I'm free until later this afternoon." He reached down and picked up Tater, and he didn't even flinch when the dog pawed a streak of mug right down the middle of his shirt. He let out a loud bark of laughter. "Can you imagine if Tater had done that to Priscilla? The top of her head would likely blow off."

Olivia frowned, praying that wasn't true. The idea that she'd get angry at them for just being dogs was horrifying. Apollo had certainly gotten into his fair share of trouble over the years, but Olivia couldn't imagine herself being angry at him just for getting her dirty.

"Oh, relax," Leo said, putting Tater into the crate. "Pris has handlers to deal with them at home. I don't know why she didn't bring them along to Christmas Grove, but it looks like she's found a way to get you to take care of them when she's otherwise engaged."

"Yeah, by threatening me. Real peach, that one," Olivia grumbled.

"Her bark is a lot bigger than her bite," he said as he loaded Scooter in with Tater.

The two dogs playfully jumped all over each other, clearly unfazed by being loaded into a crate. Olivia closed the hatch and waved at Leo as she moved to climb into the driver's seat.

Leo opened the passenger door and slid in, grinning at her.

"Whatcha doing, Leo?" Olivia asked the movie star.

"Going with you. What does it look like I'm doing?" He clipped his seatbelt in. "I thought you could show me Christmas Grove while we're waiting for Scooter and Tater to get their beauty treatments."

Olivia gaped at him, unsure why this gorgeous actor was interested in spending time with her. Though she had to admit that standing around all day while he waited for production to be ready for him had to be mind-numbingly boring. Maybe he just wanted to be entertained.

Leo reached over and put two fingers under Olivia's chin, lifting it up until her mouth closed. "Don't be so surprised that someone like me wants to spend a little time with you. If you had to hang around Hollywood types all the time, you'd understand how nice it is to spend a day with someone who isn't always trying to use you for your connections."

Olivia nodded and swallowed. "Yeah, I can see how that would be frustrating."

He shrugged. "It's all just part of the game. Most days, I handle it, but today, I'd rather take those little dogs to the groomer and maybe take a walk around this charming town with a beautiful woman."

"I seriously doubt you have problems finding beautiful women to hang out with," Olivia said as she put the car and gear.

"No, but it's not often when one isn't really interested in spending time with me. It turns out that intrigues me, Olivia Mann. *You* definitely intrigue me."

Olivia side-eyed him when she stopped to turn onto the main road. "Are you trying to flatter me, Leo?"

"You bet your pretty little bottom. Is it working?"

No. Not at all. Olivia wasn't buying his charm. She felt a little like he thought she was some sort of conquest, and there was zero chance she'd be a notch on his bedpost. "Sorry, you're going to have to work a lot harder than that, Mr. West."

Leo chuckled. "Is that a challenge, Olivia?"

"Nope. Just a fact."

CHAPTER 12

*D*eclan stood in Bark the Halls, eyeing the various Christmas-themed dog outfits. He'd been in town running errands for Payton when he'd spotted the Christmas Grinch outfits in the front window. He wasn't sure why he'd walked in, considering neither he nor his sister had a dog, but Olivia did.

And he'd already seen her dress her dog Apollo up in deer antlers. He'd be adorable as the Grinch himself.

He chuckled to himself. What was he doing? He had no idea, but he grabbed the Grinch outfit and headed to the checkout counter.

He was on his way out when he spotted Olivia's Outback pulling into the spot in front of the store. His heart jumped a bit at the idea of seeing her, and he couldn't help the smile that claimed his lips as he started to move toward her car.

Then the passenger door opened and that actor, Leo West, climbed out.

Declan stopped in his tracks and watched as Leo joined Olivia at the back of her car and pressed his hand to the small of her back. His gaze narrowed in on Leo's hand and suddenly Declan's good mood fled. He had an intense desire to walk over there and forcibly remove the man's hand from Olivia's body. But he didn't own Olivia. They weren't dating, even if they had made Priscilla believe they were. Just because they'd spent the evening together the night before, didn't mean they'd do it again.

Too bad it had been the best date of his life. Every woman he'd dated before, and likely after, would pale in comparison.

The pair unloaded Tater and Scooter and were laughing about something as they guided the dogs toward Bark the Halls. Olivia was only a foot away when she spotted Declan, causing her to stumble. He reached out for her, but Leo got there first, catching her with one arm so that she didn't land face-first on the cobblestone sidewalk.

"Whoa there," Leo said, putting her back on her feet. "Watch it. We don't want to lose Tater and Scooter again."

The two shih tzus were sitting at Leo's feet, staring up at Olivia as if they were fascinated by what was happening.

"Can you imagine if they got off their leashes on Main Street?" Olivia asked, her expression horrified.

"That's not going to happen," Leo said. "These angels aren't going to cause an issue." He crouched down and scratched their ears.

"Angels? Looks like they might have had the devil possessing them for a bit," Declan said.

Olivia laughed. "I think they might have. Little buggers

were chasing a cat and rolling around in the muddy snow this morning. I'm sure it's no surprise that Ms. Cain was less than thrilled. They're going in for a spa appointment."

Declan's gaze lingered on Olivia as he admired her dancing eyes. Despite the fact that she'd obviously been manipulated by Priscilla Cain to deal with her dogs, Olivia seemed relaxed and happy just as she had the night before when he'd shown her everything he loved about the town she called home.

Leo cleared his throat. "We better get these two girls inside so they aren't late for their appointments."

There was silence for a moment before Olivia blinked and then said, "Right. See you later, Declan."

Declan stayed rooted in his spot as he watched Olivia and the movie star walk into Bark the Halls. Olivia went in first. Leo paused for just a moment, glancing over his shoulder. He met Declan's gaze and gave him a self-satisfied look. Then with a smirk, he followed her into the store.

Clutching his shopping bag, Declan forced himself not to follow the man into Bark the Halls. He didn't have a claim on Olivia. Only a lie that they were dating. Gritting his teeth, he walked the half block to where his truck was parked and left before he could do something stupid like punch the bastard out.

After dropping off the supplies he'd picked up for his sister, Declan headed over to the inn to get to work. Thankfully, they weren't filming in his kitchen, and he was able to slip in unnoticed.

Or so he thought.

Declan was busy preparing a pan of focaccia bread when

there was a quiet knock on the kitchen door. He glanced up just as Priscilla Cain walked in, her black gown trailing behind her as the kitchen lights glittered off the jewels in her tiara.

"Hello there, Chef Declan," she said in a sugary voice.

"Ms. Cain. Is there something I can do for you?" he asked, annoyed that she was bothering him when all he wanted to do was lose himself in his job.

She sauntered over to him, her hips swaying suggestively. "I think I've made myself pretty clear about what I want. How about we stop pretending there's nothing between us so we can start having some fun? This sugarplum town is entirely too sweet for the likes of me."

"I like this sugarplum town," Declan said, ignoring her question.

"Do you like your women sweet, too?" she asked.

He raised one eyebrow at her. "You are aware that I'm dating Olivia, right?"

"I guess that answers my question." She gave him a sultry look. "If you're ever in the mood for a woman with a little more spice, you know where to find me."

"I wouldn't count on it." Declan's tone was cold and void of emotion.

Her eyes narrowed and her lips formed a tight line before she said, "I'd watch the way you talk to the star of this movie. You wouldn't want me to insist that we move locations, would you? I doubt your girlfriend would appreciate it if she lost all that revenue."

Declan wiped his hands on a towel and then pressed them against the stainless-steel counter. Staring her straight in the eyes, he said, "You might be able to use that threat to get under Olivia's skin, but I'm not intimidated by the woman who I saw making out with her costar out in the woods. I'm fairly sure you don't want the tabloids getting ahold of that. Or the fact that she hit on the chef later that same afternoon."

"You wouldn't dare," Priscilla said, her voice shaking with anger.

"Oh, but I would. Now stop threatening Olivia and learn to take no for an answer because I'm not even remotely interested in sleeping with you."

"Sleep with *you?*" she asked as if she hadn't just propositioned him a few moments before. "In your dreams." She spun around on her heel to stalk out. Just before she left, she paused and said, "Watch your back, Declan McCabe. No one threatens me and gets away with it."

Declan waited until she was gone and then snorted his derision. There was nothing Priscilla Cain could do to him. His job at the inn was safe and so was his position at the restaurant down in Napa. He'd known the owner for years. Her threats meant next to nothing to him. And if she came after Olivia, she'd find out just how far he was willing to go to protect his... friend.

CHAPTER 13

"Hot chocolate?" Leo asked Olivia as they walked past Love Potions.

"Sure." She followed the actor into the store and smiled to herself when Lily Paddington's eyes nearly bugged out.

Lily dropped the tray of chocolates she was holding and rushed over to the counter. "Mr. West. I was wondering if we'd ever see you in here. I just want you to know that *Merry Me for Christmas* is one of my favorite shows. My son and I never miss a new episode."

"Thank you. That's very kind of you to say," Leo said, holding his hand out to her.

Lily reached for his hand and then closed her eyes and practically swooned when he covered her hand with both of his.

"It's very lovely to meet you, Ms.—"

"Paddington," Olivia filled in when Lily was too starstruck to answer. "Lily Paddington."

"It's lovely to meet you, Lily Paddington," Leo said.

"Yes," Lily answered, making Olivia laugh. Lily's face turned bright red as she stammered, "I mean, it's, ah, lovely to meet you, too."

Leo grinned at her, and when she didn't let go of his hand, he gently pulled it back and then stuffed both hands in his jeans pockets.

"Oh my gosh," Lily said, shaking her head. "I'm not usually like this. It's just that it isn't every day when a movie star walks in the shop."

"I understand. It's not every day I run into someone so charming," Leo said, laying it on thick.

"Now you're just flattering me," Lily said. "You better stop or you'll have me following you around town, and I don't think the boss would take too kindly to me just leaving in the middle of my shift."

Leo chuckled. "Okay. How about I just order two hot chocolates. And if you could slip a love spell into Olivia's, I wouldn't complain."

Lily's eyebrows shot up as she glanced at Olivia. "Is he serious?"

"He better not be." Olivia glared at Leo. "Not cool, man."

"I just figured it was the only way to get you away from that chef of yours," he said with a wink.

"You and Declan are a thing?" Lily asked, her eyes wide with excitement. "Oh my gosh. Zach said he thought there was something there, but I thought he was just seeing things. This is amazing. Declan is hot."

Olivia wanted to tell Lily the truth, but with Leo standing right next to her, her only option was to let Lily keep believing she was dating her chef or let on to Leo that they'd lied. No way was she doing that. She didn't want Priscilla finding out and then thinking that Declan was fair game. "Declan and I... Well, it's new."

Lily clapped her hands together in delight and then quickly turned narrowed eyes on Leo. "And you wanted me to slip her a love potion? Shame on you."

Leo held his hands up in a surrender motion and took a step back. "Message received. I won't ever joke about that again."

"Good." Lily's smile returned as she asked, "Now, two hot chocolates. Anything else?"

"Not for me," Olivia said.

"Why don't you add in some of those Kiss Me Chocolates," Leo said, pointing at the lip shaped chocolates in the case.

"They don't really make anyone want to kiss you," Lily said. "Just in case you were thinking of slipping them to someone."

Leo smirked. "You really don't think much of me, do you, Lily Paddington?"

"That's not..." Lily shook her head and frowned. "I just wanted to be clear, that's all."

"You've been very clear," Leo said with a sharp nod. "No spelled candy without consent."

"There we go. That's what I like to hear." Lily whistled to herself as she got busy filling their order.

Leo insisted on paying and shook Lily's hand once more before they stepped back out onto Main Street.

"That was interesting," Leo said.

"Lily's a good person," Olivia said and took a sip of her hot cocoa. As always, it was rich and creamy and deliciously decadent.

"She's paranoid," he said.

Olivia turned her attention to the movie star and rolled her eyes. "Why? Because she wants to make sure no one is spelled against their will? Do you have any idea how often that happens to people? Women in particular? Lily Paddington is a good person and one of my friends. If I were you, I wouldn't say anything else about her."

Leo stared at her for a long moment and then finally nodded. "Okay. Message received."

They walked in silence down the cobblestone sidewalk.

Olivia glanced at her phone, checking the time, wishing it was time to pick up Tater and Scooter. Leo West could be charming when he wanted to, but he also got under her skin with his arrogance. The way he'd talked about Lily had really upset her.

"I think I might owe you an apology," Leo said.

"What gave it away?" she asked, not bothering to hide the frustration in her tone.

"That." He paused and reached out for her hand. "I didn't mean to upset you."

"That's not an apology, Leo. And honestly, it doesn't really matter. Just try not to be an entitled jerk next time."

He let out a huff of disbelief and then chuckled to himself. "You're something else, Olivia Mann. I don't think I've ever met someone quite like you before."

"Why? Because I called you out on your BS?" she asked.

"Yes. No one really does that."

"Then you're lucky you met me, aren't you?" She gave him a tiny smile and then stepped past him as she headed toward the town square.

Leo fell into step beside her. "I'm beginning to think that I am, in fact, very lucky I met you."

Olivia wasn't sure if he was being sincere or if he was just laying on that charm again, but it didn't really matter. There wasn't ever going to be anything between them other than friendship.

"Hey, look at that," Leo said, pointing toward a horseless carriage. "How about you show me your town in one of those?"

"Um, I don't think so," Olivia said, not wanting to do anything to tarnish the memory of the night before with Declan. "It's a much better ride at night when the lights are all lit up."

"Shall we make it a date?" he asked.

"Leo, what did I tell you about me and Declan?"

"Oh, right. Well, how about I take you to lunch then? A woman has to eat, right?"

"She does," Olivia agreed and followed him as he made his way to Mistletoe's, a bistro that was a farm-to-table establishment.

The moment they sat down, Olivia wished she'd declined the invitation. Leo took it upon himself to order for both of them, including a couple of glasses of wine even though she'd declined, stating that she still had work to do back at the inn.

"It's just one glass, Olivia. Everyone has drinks with lunch," he insisted.

"I don't."

Leo gazed at her with that assumed-disbelief expression again and said, "This is what I like about you. Sass. I love the sass."

"I'm glad I can entertain," she said and took a bite of her pork belly. Even though she'd been annoyed when he'd ordered for them, she had to admit that the dish was delicious. More than that, it was droolworthy. "You know what, Leo?"

"What's that?" he asked, holding his fork up.

"You can order for me any time you want to. Everything on this plate is making me happy."

"Does that mean there's going to be a repeat of this?" he asked hopefully.

"What do you mean by *this*? Lunch?" she asked.

"A date, Olivia. Maybe you've heard of them? They're when two people go out on the town, usually something like dinner and a movie."

She shook her head. "Nice try. No date, but we can keep the door open for lunch the next time we need to take Tater and Scooter into town to get groomed."

"Then I'll pencil you in," he said and literally wrote a note on a napkin and stuffed it into his pocket. "I'm holding you to that."

"I'd expect nothing less."

By the time they were done with lunch, it was time to pick up Tater and Scooter. Once they had them loaded in the car and were on their way back to the inn, Leo reached over and squeezed her hand. "Thank you for showing me your town. I liked seeing it through your eyes."

Olivia nodded, but inside, all she could think about was that she hadn't shown him her town. Not the parts she loved. Because all of those places now belonged to her and Declan.

CHAPTER 14

"*H*ow was your date?" Declan asked Olivia that afternoon when she walked into the kitchen.

She tilted her head to the side, studying him. "What date?"

Declan scowled to himself as he kept his attention on the tomatoes he was slicing. "The one you had with the movie star this afternoon."

When she didn't answer, he glanced up to find her smirking at him. "What?"

"You're jealous."

"No, I'm not." The denial rolled right off his tongue as if he were a world class liar. "What exactly would I be jealous about?"

That made her laugh. "If you say so, Declan. But for the record, it wasn't a date. I was taking Tater and Scooter to get cleaned up and Leo asked to come along because he was bored. What was I supposed to say? No? That would've been unnecessarily rude, don't you think?"

"He overstepped." Declan was aware he was being petulant, but he just couldn't seem to stop himself. He was jealous. It wasn't an emotion he was used to dealing with.

"How?" She placed her hands on her hips and gave him a pointed stare.

"As far as he knows, we're dating. It's not cool to make a move on someone who's already otherwise committed."

Olivia pursed her lips as she considered his argument. He was sure she was going to put him in his place. Tell him he was the one overstepping a boundary. After all, he didn't really have any business worrying about how she spent her time. But when she spoke, she said, "You're right about that. And he did make comments that indicated he was interested in me. Or at least interested enough to flirt with me. But don't worry. I turned him down gently."

Declan swallowed a very caveman response and nodded. "That's good. Or at least it is if you aren't actually interested in him." As soon as the words left his mouth, Declan wanted to kick himself. Why was he being a complete idiot when it came to Olivia?

Chuckling again, she shook her head. "How about we stop talking about Leo West and move on to whatever it is you're making? It looks delicious."

Turning his attention to the food in front of him, he said, "It's caprese salad to go with the chicken pesto and sundried tomato pasta. It's tonight's meal for the crew."

She let out a little moan, indicating her approval.

Declan wanted desperately to hear that sound again,

preferably when they were alone. He cleared his throat, trying to force the inappropriate thoughts out of his head and said, "I got something for you while I was in town."

"You did?" she asked, sounding surprised. "Why?"

"Because I saw it and thought of you. Or more accurately, I thought of Apollo." He gestured to the bag that was sitting on a shelf behind him. "Go on. Open it."

"You got Apollo a present?" she asked as she reached for the bag.

He didn't answer as he waited to see her reaction.

The moment she peeked into the bag, her entire face lit up with delight. "Declan!" She pulled the costume out and held it up, admiring it. "You got Apollo a Grinch outfit?"

"I saw it in the window and just thought..." He shrugged one shoulder. "It was an impulse purchase."

"It's perfect! Thank you." Olivia leaned over and gave him a kiss on his cheek. "I can't wait to see him running around in this." Her laugh was high-pitched and full of joy. "You'll come by my apartment after you're done here so you can see him, right?"

"Uh, sure. If you want me to," he said, placing the last of the tomatoes onto the platter.

"I insist." She glanced at the tray in front of them. "Did you by chance make enough for us to steal some of this for dinner? I have wine."

Had she just invited him over for dinner? More accurately, she'd invited him to bring her dinner, but he didn't mind. Not at all. "Sure. Don't I always?"

"Good. I'm going to go check and make sure production doesn't need anything else from me and then

I'm going to take Apollo out. Just come by when you're ready."

She grabbed the bag that contained Apollo's costume and then practically bounced out of the kitchen.

As Declan watched her go, her infectious joy washed over him and made him feel lighter than he had in weeks. Maybe even months. All because he'd bought a silly costume for her beloved dog. If that was all it took, he had a feeling he'd be spending a lot more cash at Bark the Halls.

When Declan was done for the day, he packed up their dinner and headed to Olivia's apartment.

She answered the door wearing leggings and an oversized T-shirt. Her slightly wavy hair was down, and Declan had an intense desire to run his fingers through her locks. He stood there staring at her like a lovesick idiot until she said, "Declan? Are you coming in?"

"Uh, yes. Of course." He followed her into her cozy space.

Apollo came running, his tail wagging. The freshly groomed dog jumped up on Declan's leg, demanding attention.

Declan handed the food to Olivia and bent to pet Apollo. "Hey there, handsome. You sure are friendly tonight."

Apollo ran around in a circle before hurling himself at Declan again.

"I can see you get no attention at all. You poor, neglected creature. Is that why you're not wearing your new Christmas outfit? Was your mom just too busy to help you try it on?"

"Oh for the love of…" Olivia rolled her eyes as she shook

her head. "He's not wearing his outfit because I just spent the last hour grooming him. He got a fresh shave, a bath, and a blow-out. You should've seen him eating it up. If there is one thing Apollo doesn't lack, it's attention."

"I see," Declan said, still talking to the dog. "You're a lucky man, you know that right? To have a woman like your mom fawning all over you is a privilege. I hope you gave her lots of love for her efforts."

Apollo dropped to the floor and rolled over onto his back, showing Declan his belly.

Declan didn't hesitate to rub the Lhasa's belly, sending the dog into obvious euphoria.

"He's a whore for belly rubs," Olivia said. "Now that he knows you're a sucker, he'll be doing that to you all night."

"I don't mind," Declan said. "He's a sweetheart."

"Yes, he is." Olivia watched the scene with a soft expression. Her lips curved into a secret smile as she walked over to her open kitchen and started dishing up their dinner. "Does the pasta need to be heated?"

"Yes," Declan confirmed. He scratched Apollo's ears and continued to heap praised on him. Finally, he stood and asked Olivia, "Where's his Grinch costume?"

She used a fork to point in the direction of an end table where she'd left the bag from Bark the Halls.

"Will Apollo mind if I put it on him?" Declan asked.

"To be honest, I'm not sure. He can be finicky when he's in a mood, but he sure seems happy with you at the moment," she said through laughter.

The dog had dropped to Declan's feet and was on his back again, wiggling around with his paws in the air.

"You're a clown," Declan said as he grabbed the bag and pulled out the costume. "Are you ready to model your new outfit for your mom?"

Apollo turned his head in Olivia's direction as if contemplating the question. Then he suddenly got to his feet and stood very still as Declan put him in the Grinch costume. When Declan had the pup velcroed in, he said, "Go on. Go show your mom how cute you are."

Olivia tore her gaze away from the French bread she was slicing to give Apollo her full attention. When she spotted the fluff ball running in her direction, she let out a happy gasp and covered her mouth with one hand. "Oh my gosh, Apollo. You are freakin' adorbs."

She fished her phone out of her pocket and took about a hundred pictures of her dog and then gave him a treat for being such a good sport. She finally glanced at Declan, her eyes shining with happiness. "He looks like such a little trouble maker. Anytime I'm stressed about anything, I'm going to put this on him and just laugh and laugh. I can't believe how ridiculous he looks. It's a good think he's such a ham, otherwise I think he'd hate us."

"I imagine a lot of dogs would. But it looks like yours is a special case," Declan said.

"He definitely is." She gestured to the table she'd set while he was busy playing with Apollo. "Have a seat. I just need to open the wine and then we're ready."

"I'll get it." Declan reached for bottle and held out his hand for the opener. A few seconds later, he poured them both a glass before they both took a seat at the table. He picked up his glass and raised it in a toast. "To the best dog in the world."

Olivia grinned. "And to the most amazing chef a girl could ask for."

"Is that what I am? Just your personal chef?" he asked playfully.

"No, not *just* my chef. You're also my dog's new best friend. And my fake boyfriend. It seems you're good for multiple roles in my life."

Declan clinked his glass to hers as he said, "To me and Apollo then, I guess."

"Definitely toast worthy." She touched her glass to his and then while holding his gaze, she took a long sip of her wine.

He followed her lead, and as he sipped the wine, all he could think about was how much he enjoyed being with her and that when Payton was fully recovered, he was going to loathe leaving for Napa. An ache suddenly formed over his heart, making him rub absently at his chest.

Olivia's brows pinched as she watched him. "Declan, are you okay?"

"Yeah, sure," he forced out, his voice huskier than usual. "Why?"

Her glaze flickered to his hand still rubbing at his chest. "You look like you might be in pain."

He stilled his hand immediately, realizing that the ache wasn't on the surface. It was deeper than that. And not something that could be fixed by medical intervention. No, this was an ache caused by the idea of leaving Christmas Grove. Or more accurately, leaving Olivia. "I'm fine," he insisted and turned his attention to the pasta. When he glanced up, he forced a smile. "Just a long day."

"You're not wrong about that." She took another long sip of her wine. "I won't be sorry when this film business is over."

Taken off guard, Declan choked on his sip of wine.

"Oh no." Olivia pounded on his back until he got himself under control. "Was it something I said?" she asked with her eyebrows raised.

"Nope. Just went down the wrong pipe," he said, wiping at his eyes. "I'm fine. Really."

She nodded and then continued her thoughts about the movie. "The disruption to operations is one thing. But dealing with a bunch of demanding Hollywood stars just takes it out of me. Could you imagine dating one of them?"

"Honestly, no. Does this mean Leo West has no chance with you?" he asked and then held his breath as he waited for her answer.

CHAPTER 15

Olivia stared at Declan. What was that question about? She knew he'd shown jealous tendencies when it came to her spending any time with Leo, but she thought that had more to do with the way the man flirted with her. But now she could see that he might actually be worried that she liked him.

"Never mind," Declan said. "It's none of my business."

"Not even while you're playing the role of my fake boyfriend?" she asked just to see what he'd say.

"We can come clean if you want to," he said as he studied his plate. "It's not really fair of me to hold you to that just so I have an excuse to dodge Priscilla."

"No way! I'm not throwing you to that she-wolf. Besides, there's no reason to. I'm not interested in Leo West. You of all people should understand why."

"Because Leo would never settle down in a place like Christmas Grove," he said, his tone flat and void of emotion.

Olivia frowned. "That's true enough. But it's not the only reason."

"No? What's the other reason?"

She sat back, holding her wine glass as she contemplated telling him the whole truth. Finally, she said, "First of all, I'm interested in being someone's first priority. Do you think an actor, especially one of his stature, has room to put a relationship first over a movie career?"

"Probably not, but that could be a pretty big generalization," he said as he leaned back and crossed his arms over his chest.

That made her laugh. "Have you met Leo? Even when he tries to do something nice for someone, it's still really all about him. And I'm not saying that as some sort of criticism. It's just that for so long, everyone in his life has revolved around him. I don't even think he realizes he's doing it, but he's come to expect it. Like today when we were out, we had lunch, and instead of letting me order for myself, he took it upon himself to order for us without even asking. Who does that?"

"Leo West, apparently," Declan said, looking a lot more interested in this conversation.

"I don't know if it was because he was trying to impress me or if he just needed to feel in control, but it's not a way to my heart. I need someone who cares about what I want." She paused and even though the words got caught in her throat, she finally forced out, "Someone like you."

Declan's defenses slipped away, leaving him with a soft expression and a vulnerability she'd never seen before. He reached over and covered her hand with his. Squeezing her fingers, he said, "I wish I was the man for you, Olivia. But we both know I have a job waiting for me in Napa when my sister gets back on her feet."

Olivia's heart was nearly beating out of her chest when she said, "Does it really have to be all or nothing? This thing that's between us... Can't we just enjoy it while we have a chance?"

Declan sucked in a sharp breath as he stared at Olivia, his gaze boring into hers.

The silence was overwhelming. Olivia clutched her now empty wine glass and wished she was holding the bottle instead. Downing it seemed like a really good idea at the moment.

But when Declan stood and gently took the glass out of her hand, all thoughts of drowning herself in wine fled. All she wanted was the man standing in front of her. The one who was looking at her with a mix of awe and tenderness.

He held his hand out to her.

Olivia took it, letting him tug her to her feet.

"Are you positive this is what you want? That you want me even if it's only for a few months?"

"Yes," Olivia whispered, knowing she'd rather have this experience even if it meant it was temporary. She'd suffered heartbreak before. At least this time she'd be left with memories she could cherish.

Declan pulled her in close and cupped one cheek as he smiled down at her. "You have no idea how much I've wanted this."

"I think I do," she said softly.

"Then you won't mind if I kiss you now?"

"Do you really have to ask?"

His lips curved up into a half smile and then he dipped his head, stopping just before his lips brushed over hers.

"What are you waiting for?" she asked breathlessly.

"You. Close the distance, Olivia. Show me that you're sure. That you really want me. That you want this."

She didn't hesitate. Every cell in her body screamed for her to finally give herself over to the magic that sparked between them. With her lips slightly parted, Olivia closed the distance between them.

The moment her lips touched his, both of his arms wrapped around her, enveloping her into his muscular frame. She let herself get completely lost in him, relishing his touch, his taste, his everything.

"Olivia," he whispered as he turned his head and trailed kisses along her jawline.

"Yes." She didn't even know what she was saying yes to. All she knew was that she wanted everything he had to give.

"We should make cookies."

Olivia froze and then stepped back, staring up at him like he'd lost his mind. "What did you just say?"

He ran a hand down his face and chuckled awkwardly. "That's not... That's not what I was going to say."

Leaning against the table, Olivia clasped her hands in front of her and waited for him to continue.

Declan stepped back into her personal space and ran gentle hands up and down her arms. "The truth is that the only thing I want to do is carry you into your bedroom and strip every last bit of clothing off that gorgeous body of yours."

"But?"

"Son of a..." He shook his head. "This is stupid. I can't believe I'm about to say this, but I don't want to rush it and end up with one of us regretting this."

"You mean you think *I'll* regret it," she said, frustrated but also touched.

"Well, no," he said. "I just don't want that to be a possibility considering five minutes ago we were fake dating and then we were eating each other's faces."

"Charming description," she said dryly and took his hand in hers as she tugged him toward her bedroom.

He stood his ground, refusing to move, but when her determined gaze met his, he just nodded once and followed her into her bedroom. "I guess this means you've thought it over."

"Declan, I've been thinking it over for weeks now." She stood in front of him, her fingers already working the buttons open on his shirt. "This isn't a five second decision. And for the record?"

He watched her expert fingers work their way through two buttons. "Yes?"

"When I make up my mind about something, it's a very rare occasion when I reconsider. I already know what it's like to share a bed with you. Trust me when I say I won't change my mind about this. Understand?"

"Completely."

"Good. Now kiss me like you mean it."

∽

OLIVIA STOOD *in an unfamiliar living room with two floor-to-ceiling glass walls that looked out over a snow-covered knoll. Below the house, there was a small picturesque city that was quiet in the early morning light. Soft classical Christmas music played from the radio as the sound of heavy footsteps clomped on the stairs.*

A girl no older than thirteen with strawberry blond hair piled in a messy bun came running down the stairs with a chocolate brown shih tzu right behind her. She rushed into the living room, paused as she stared at the tree and the one gift that was wrapped beneath it, and then hurried into the kitchen calling, "Mom? Dad?"

There was no answer, just an echo off the walls.

She frowned and then walked slowly to the refrigerator and plucked the handwritten note from beneath a magnet.

It read:

Priscilla,

Sorry, honey. Your dad and I were called into work. It's a PR emergency. Go ahead and open your gift. It's under the tree. We'll have Christmas dinner when we get home.

Merry Christmas,

Mom

The note slipped from Priscilla's fingertips as her eyes turned glassy with tears. The dog pressed its tiny body against her leg, prompting her to pick up the dog and bury her face in her fur as she sobbed.

Olivia tried to reach out to her, but when she placed a soft hand on the girl's shoulder, it was clear she hadn't felt it.

"Priscilla?" Olivia tried.

Still no answer.

The air around Olivia seemed to be electrically charged before there was a tiny flash of light, and suddenly the adult version of Priscilla was standing right beside her. "I can't hear you."

Startled, Olivia jumped slightly. "Where did you come from?"

She shrugged. "How should I know?"

Olivia eyed the woman beside her and then the young girl who was sitting in front of the tree with her dog, holding the package. Tears stained her cheeks, but she'd stopped crying and now just seemed resigned. Olivia turned to the woman standing beside her. "That's you, right?"

"Yep. My thirteenth birthday is in six days," she said with a sigh. "Not that anyone will remember."

Sadness hit Olivia squarely in the gut. No kid deserved that. What kind of parents did that to a kid? "Did your parents really go to work on Christmas day?"

"They were always working. Doing PR for entitled Hollywood stars meant they showed up when they were called, no matter what else was happening. I think that year, their biggest client was trying to climb down the chimney and got stuck. They had to spin the story as something other than what actually happened."

"He didn't get stuck in the chimney?"

"Oh, he did. But it wasn't to act as Santa. His wife hid their drugs there, and he was trying to find them."

That sounded more plausible than a man getting dressed in a Santa suit and actually trying to slide down the chimney. "Did both of them have to go? I can't believe they left you by yourself on Christmas morning."

Priscilla turned to Olivia. "I'm not alone. Luna is there with me." She nodded to the shih tzu. "Dogs are the only beings on earth that one can count on."

While Olivia could understand why Priscilla would say that, she knew it wasn't true. Not everyone was like Priscilla's workaholic parents. But instead of pointing that out, Olivia watched as Priscilla walked over to her younger self. The older version rested a hand on her younger self's shoulder as the young girl carefully unwrapped the present as if it were a prized possession.

When young Priscilla opened the box and pulled out a pair of puppy slippers, she stared at them for a long moment, then put them on her feet before she picked up her dog and walked back upstairs.

Christmas was over.

The older Priscilla snapped her fingers and suddenly the scene changed. They were standing in a bedroom that was decorated in bright red satin fabrics. Posters of glamorous Hollywood icons adorned the walls and in the corner, there was a makeup vanity complete with a lighted mirror and rows and rows of expensive makeup.

The door opened and a teenage version of Priscilla walked in with the same dog on her heels. Her hair and makeup were done up to perfection, but she wore sweats under a robe and the same dog slippers she'd gotten for Christmas about five years ago.

"Ah, this is an interesting Christmas," Priscilla said. "Finally one when the parents are home. That was the year I learned that I actually didn't want to be with them on Christmas. Not the way they celebrated."

"How was that?" Olivia asked.

"You'll see."

There was a loud knock on teenage Priscilla's door. "Pris, come down. The guests are here."

128

"I'm not coming," the teenager called back.

The doorknob rattled and the pounding started again. "You know who's down there, Priscilla. This meeting is very important to your father and me. Now open your door and let's go celebrate Christmas."

"Meeting." The teenager snorted. "I'm not spending my Christmas sucking up to the studio execs just so you and dad can get your precious Millie and Chaz roles in their next big movies. That's not my idea of family time."

"It's good for you, too, baby. Remember, the success from the show you're on isn't going to last forever. You need these contacts," her mother reasoned.

"I don't need anything." Priscilla put a pair of headphones on and rolled over on her bed away from the door. Her dog crawled up next to her and put her head on the pillow right next to Priscilla's.

There was more pounding on the door and pleading until finally her mother cursed her daughter and told her that the career she'd work so hard for would crash and burn just as soon as this show ended, because she'd do everything in her power to make sure her ungrateful daughter learned what happened when a client was disloyal.

Her mother pounded on the door one last time before she left the teenager alone on Christmas... again.

"That was the last year I lived in their house," present day Priscilla said. "I left a week later when I turned eighteen."

"Did you ever talk to them again?"

Priscilla turned to Olivia and opened her mouth to answer, but there was a scream and another pounding on the door that sent Olivia sitting bolt upright in bed, her eyes blurry from sleep.

"What's happening?" Olivia said, her voice raspy. She rubbed at her gritty eyes, trying to focus in the early morning light.

Declan leaned over and quickly kissed her on the cheek before he slid out of bed and pulled on his jeans. "No idea. I'll go check it out."

"Wait!" Olivia called, but it was too late. Declan had already slipped into the other room. She scrambled out of bed and quickly threw on a pair of jeans and a T-shirt before she ran out into her living room to find Priscilla standing in her doorway, her hair plastered to her head with what looked and smelled like… mayonnaise? Was she doing some sort of hair treatment?

"You!" Priscilla pointed at Olivia. "What kind of establishment are you running?" She held up a small bottle of shampoo and then threw it at Olivia.

Olivia moved to catch it, but she'd been too caught off guard and the bottle tumbled to the floor. It hit hard and the thick creamy substance splattered all over her hardwood floor. The vinegar scent washed over her and it was then that Olivia confirmed that it was in fact mayonnaise.

"Look at what your maid service did to my hair!" Priscilla screamed, pointing at her shiny locks. "What am I going to do now? I can't film today after this."

"I…" Olivia cleared her throat. "I don't think anyone would intentionally sabotage your shampoo bottles, but if they did, I swear to you that I'll get to the bottom of it."

"That doesn't help me today, now does it?" she said, her eyes full of fury.

"Can't you just wash it out?" Olivia asked. Was there

something special about mayo? Olivia hadn't ever tried any of those home treatments. She wasn't sure what the pitfalls were.

"No, genius. Not when my shampoo has been replaced with this garbage."

"I have some shampoo. Let me just—"

"My hair care products are top of the line. I'm certain your dollar store, generic brand isn't going to give me the shine I need for the cameras."

Maybe not, but the mayonnaise probably would. "I'll go out and get you a new bottle. Just tell Declan what it is and—"

"It's only available in France," Priscilla said with a sniff. "The soonest it can get here with expedited international shipping is by next week. Until then, you'll need to go to the nearest beauty supply place and pick up a bottle of both shampoo and conditioner by the name brand London Rain. Bring your credit card. You're going to need it. And if whoever did this isn't fired by the end of the day, I'll be writing that review on my website explaining that the proprietor not only hires thieves, but also sleeps with the help. Can you imagine how that will go over in this political climate?"

"Priscilla, there's no need—"

"I'm done talking to you. Do your job or I'll put you out of business." She spun and stalked out.

Declan waited a moment before he slammed the door, shutting out the harsh reality that half the production crew had overheard Priscilla's threats and accusation.

Without a word, Declan walked over and wrapped Olivia in his arms. He pressed a soft kiss to her forehead and said, "Just think. In two months, you'll not only be rid of me, but you'll also never have to see the dragon lady again."

Olivia clutched at him, wishing she was back in bed, cuddled up next to him. "That's not as comforting as you think," she muttered into his bare chest.

"Yeah, I guess it isn't," he whispered, caressing her hair. "Listen, I know you have a crisis on your hands, but what do you think about getting a quick shower before we face this day?"

She knew she should decline, but she just couldn't force herself. After the dream she'd had, combined with the reality of dealing with Priscilla Cain, she needed a shower more than she'd ever needed one in her life. She could think of nothing better than sharing that shower with Declan McCabe.

CHAPTER 16

*D*eclan sat with Apollo out in the garden, both of them with their faces tilted to the sun. It was a cold day, but Declan barely felt it. He could still feel the heat of having Olivia in his arms the night before. Everything about their evening had been perfect. He'd fallen asleep with her in his arms, exactly as he'd dreamed ever since they'd parted ways in San Francisco six months ago.

He'd realized then that he'd never wanted to let her go. And that was why he'd been so irritated when he'd woken that last morning and found her gone. He'd spent years being the one who left first and had never thought twice. But the one time it'd happened to him, he'd been gutted. Though he hadn't admitted it to himself. No, he'd pretended it was all fine… right up until he'd walked back into her life all because his sister had begged him for help.

Apollo jumped up on the bench Declan was sitting on and rested his head in Declan's lap. As he caressed the dog's ear, he wondered how he was going to walk out of Olivia's life once his sister was back on the job. Would he be ready to go in two months, or was he only going to get more attached to the gorgeous raven-haired beauty?

He truly had no idea.

The sound of raised voices drew his attention to the front of the inn, and he wondered if he should see what was happening. Olivia had hurried into town to find the hair care products that Priscilla had demanded. If there was an altercation, someone needed to handle it.

But just as he was about to move Apollo, the voices stopped and Leo West stalked around the side of the inn, running a frustrated hand through his hair. When he looked up and saw Declan, he paused. But then a moment later, he pasted on a cocky smile and said, "You do realize that when I set my sights on a woman, I never lose that battle, right? Olivia might be dating you now, but that won't last long."

Declan eyed the actor as he leaned against a tree trunk and stuffed his hands into his front pockets. Even though it was barely eight in the morning, he was dressed in a dark suit with a pink pinstriped button-down shirt, suspenders, and a bright pink tie. He was holding a cup of coffee and looked like a poster boy for the LA metrosexual. "There is no fight, Leo. Olivia has already made her choice. She's with me."

"We'll see about that. When's the last time you had to compete with a guy who has been at the top of the Sexiest Man Alive list."

Declan let out a humorless laugh. "If you think Olivia cares about that, you have no idea who she is."

Leo seemed to contemplate that bit of information and then nodded thoughtfully. "Yeah. That sounds like Olivia. Honestly, that's why I like her so much. She's very much her own person, not at all interested in riding someone else's coattails. That's the appeal."

"*That's* the appeal?" Declan echoed. "You're saying you want to date her because she isn't a gold digger?" He shook his head, comforted in the fact that the man hadn't taken any time at all to understand her. "Good luck, man. You're gonna need it."

Declan placed Apollo down on the ground and then said, "Come on, buddy. I'll get you a treat before I head into the kitchen."

"She deserves better than what you can give her," Leo said.

Pausing mid-step, Declan looked back at the man. "Are you talking about me or you?"

The movie star opened his mouth to speak but then closed it and walked away without answering Declan's question.

"Looks like I hit a nerve," Declan said to Apollo. The dog let out a little bark of agreement, and the two of them walked back into the inn together. Before he could open Olivia's door for Apollo, he spotted Priscilla dressed in a black lace corset dress and lace-up boots. Her hair was magically back to its soft red waves. It didn't escape his notice that her mystical-woman look was in direct contrast with Leo's hipster theme. He wondered what the director had in mind.

He was about to ask what their scene was about but

stopped when he noticed the deep sadness in her eyes. "Priscilla, is everything all right?"

She jerked her head up, obviously startled. She hadn't even heard him enter the reception area. "Sorry, I didn't see you there." She averted her gaze and said, "I'm fine. Just getting into character."

Declan didn't believe her for a minute, but it wasn't his place to press her for details. Whatever she was going through, it was none of his business. "Okay. Let me know if there's anything you need."

She turned her attention back to him, studying him with detached interest. "Do you have family, Declan?"

He was taken aback by her question, but quickly recovered and nodded. "Yes. A sister. And my mom."

"Are you close?"

He wondered where this was coming from, but decided it didn't matter. Priscilla seemed like she could use someone to talk to. It might as well be him. "I am with my sister. Not so much with my mom." He walked over to her and gestured to the chair beside her. "Mind if I sit?"

"Only if you let me pet your dog."

"Sure, but he's not mine. That's Apollo. He's Olivia's."

"Really? I guess she's not quite as bad as I thought she was." The actress put her hand out for Apollo so that he could give it a sniff.

It only took a few seconds before he was lying down and showing her his belly.

"You are such a traitor," Declan said with a shake of his head. "You'll take belly rubs from anyone who will offer them up, won't you, A-man?"

The dog put his paws in the air and gave Priscilla a look of pure adoration as she used her long nails to scratch his belly.

"This is what I love about dogs," Priscilla said. "They're so uncomplicated. If you pay attention, you always know what they need."

It might have been the first thing the woman had ever said that Declan agreed with. "I agree. Apollo is particularly transparent. For him, it's belly rubs, treats, and ear scratches. Not necessarily in that order."

"Can't say I blame him," she said with a soft smile. When Apollo had enough, he flipped back over onto his belly and scooted over so that he was lying on one of Priscilla's boots. "Gosh, you're too adorable for your own good."

"It's all part of his charm," Declan agreed. "But he's not the only ham in this joint. What are your two balls of fluff up to? Napping in your room?"

"They better be. Those trouble-makers," she said with a laugh. "I've never met two other shih tzus that get into so much trouble. I mean, how exactly do they manage to escape their crates all the time? It's not just here. They do it at home, too. I swear they've conjured up some spell that enables them to unlock those doors."

Declan raised both eyebrows. "Are you confessing that Tater and Scooter are known escape artists, and yet you blame Olivia for their shenanigans?"

She opened her mouth to say something, but then closed it and shook her head. "I think I'd better plead the fifth."

Declan let out a loud bark of laughter. At least she was being honest. "I see."

She chuckled and he wondered if that was the first time he'd heard a real laugh from her. It made her entire face light up.

"You should laugh more. It looks good on you."

Priscilla met his gaze, scrutinizing him as if searching for some other meaning to his words. When she didn't seem to find anything, her expression softened and she said, "Thanks. I'll try."

A lull fell between them, and Declan had just about decided it was time to go when she said, "I don't talk to my parents."

He didn't miss the slight note of pain in her tone, and he gave her his full attention. "Any reason in particular?"

"They don't really care about me. All they care about is using me to further their careers."

"I'm sorry," Declan said, meaning it. No matter how awful Priscilla had acted for the past few weeks, she still didn't deserve to have her own parents use her. "That's rough. How long has that been going on?"

"Since I was fourteen. That's when I landed my first movie role." She sighed. "Christmas is always a rough time for me. I usually take time off to regroup, but the production company wanted this film to be as authentic as possible, so here we are filming a Christmas movie that won't even come out until next year. I'm just finding it hard to find any sort of Christmas spirit." She glanced down at her outfit. "It's pretty fitting that they've dressed me up as the angel of death, don't you think?"

"Is that your real character or one you just made up because you're in black, *again*?" Declan asked.

Priscilla waved a hand as if to wave away the question. "It doesn't matter. It's how I feel most days anyway. Especially now that I've scuttled my Christmas plans."

"Which plans were those? Were you headed anywhere interesting?" Declan didn't particularly like Priscilla, but he had to admit that he was a little stunned she was opening up to him. He had a hunch she didn't talk to many people. Not about anything real. And he felt obligated to keep the conversation going as long as she was a willing participant. Maybe he'd find out why she was so prickly all the time.

"Up to the Pacific Northwest. A small town called Befana Bay. I bet you've never heard of it," she said with a smirk.

"Can't say I have. Were you going to visit friends there?"

"Something like that. But now me and the girls can just stay here. Maybe go snowshoeing. Or ice skating. Something physical instead of standing around all day waiting for the shoot to start."

"Your dogs ice skate?" he asked just to break the mood.

"Huh?" She looked confused for a moment, and then she realized he was just messing with her. "You're a troublemaker yourself, Declan. You know that, right?" she said, her eyes glinting with amusement.

"I've been told that once or twice," Declan said. "It's all in good fun."

Her phone beeped, and after she looked at it, she groaned. "Work calls." She petted Apollo one last time and started to walk off. She got three steps before she turned around and said, "Listen, I know you're dating Ms. Mann, but I really enjoyed our talk. Do you mind if we get together for coffee or lunch sometime? Just platonic. I promise. That whole dating thing just hasn't been working out for me."

Declan hesitated, wondering what Olivia would think of this arrangement. But then, did it matter? They were temporary. Hadn't made each other any promises. And it was just an hour at a café. No big deal. "Sure," he said.

"Coffee it is then. Tomorrow at eight?" Priscilla asked him.

"Coffee at eight," he agreed and then closed his eyes and sucked in a deep breath. Who was he kidding? Olivia would not take kindly to him slipping out of her bed to go meet her least favorite person for coffee.

"Was that you chatting with the dragon lady?" Olivia asked from behind him.

Declan suppressed a grimace and turned around to greet his favorite person. "She wanted to say hi to Apollo. What could I do? His charm is just too much for the ladies to resist."

"Ha! You got that right." She bent down and gave Apollo a scratch, causing him to once again roll onto his back and demand belly rubs. Which he got, because no one could refuse his furry butt.

When Olivia straightened, Declan took her hand and said, "Come with me."

"Where are we going?" she asked with a chuckle.

"To finally make those cookies. I hope you're ready to make magic."

"With you?" she asked. "Always."

CHAPTER 17

"What do you want me to make?" Declan asked, flipping open his recipe book. "Any requests?"

Olivia peered over his shoulder, eyeing the various holiday cookie recipes he'd collected over the years. "Something with marshmallows. Wouldn't you just love to see Priscilla deal with that gooey stuff on national television?"

"Evil. Pure evil," he said with a snicker. "Though it does serve her right after she ordered you to come up with cookies choices for that baking show. I have a marshmallow and caramel recipe in here. That would really stick it to her. Get it? Stick it to her?"

Groaning, Olivia gave him a playful shrug. "I didn't realize I was going to have to endure your dad jokes. But I do like the way you think. What else can we throw at her?

What about chocolate-dipped, cream-stuffed cookies? Or raspberry sandwich cookies?"

"What are you trying to do to me?" Declan asked. "Keep me locked in the kitchen all day until I dehydrate and pass out from starvation? None of those are simple. You know that, right?"

"We can't give Priscilla Cain a simple recipe. She'd rip us a new one. Can you imagine her showing up on the show with a simple gingerbread recipe?" Olivia already figured that no matter what cookie they presented to the woman, she was going to complain. At least if they gave her fancy looking ones, she couldn't accuse them of trying to sabotage her just because Olivia was competing, too.

"Fine, but I'm going to need your help," Declan said, already pulling dry ingredients off his shelves.

"Happy to." She pressed up onto her tip toes and went in to give him a kiss on the cheek, but he turned toward her and caught her lips instead. Before she knew what she was doing, she had her arms around him and everything else faded away as the kiss deepened. There were no cookies. No inn. No movie being made. It was just Olivia and Declan.

When Declan eventually pulled back, Olivia just stood there, staring up at him as if she were in a haze.

He chuckled. "I don't think we're going to get these cookies made if you keep staring at me like that."

"Cookies?" she muttered as the realization dawned on her, and she quickly took a step back. "For the love of the goddess," she said, frowning. "Why does my brain turn into total mush when you're kissing me?"

Declan rewarded her with a cocky smile. When he opened his mouth to speak, she put a hand up, stopping him.

"Never mind. That was a rhetorical question. Come on. Let's just get to work."

Olivia was surprised to find that they worked well together in the kitchen. Since she was hardly the expert, she played the role of Declan's assistant until eventually all the cookies were baked and were cooling on racks.

"Do you mind if I make one more batch of cookies?" Olivia asked him. "I just want to do a test run for the ones I'm going to make on the show. It's been a number of years, and I want to make sure I haven't forgotten anything."

"Of course not," Declan said, testing one of the cookies to see if they were cool yet. "How about we switch roles and I'll assist you. What are we making?"

Olivia bit down on her bottom lip. "Sugar cookies."

He watched her for a moment, and she wondered if he thought she was joking.

"They're simple, but the way I decorate them, they get a lot of compliments. I figure that on a show, presentation matters."

"That's true enough," he said with a nod. "Sugar cookies it is. I can't wait to see how you decorate these."

"It'll be worth it. I promise."

A couple hours later, with four batches of cookies done, Olivia and Declan's aprons were smeared with chocolate, raspberry, sticky marshmallow, streaks of caramel, and blue and white icing.

"I guess we shot ourselves in the foot when we chose

these recipes," Olivia said, shaking her head at herself. That's what she got for being petty.

"Maybe, but they turned out really fantastic," Declan said, waving at the rows of holiday goodness. "And yours are gorgeous."

Olivia had cut out round sugar cookies and smaller pieces that were in the shape of a base and had turned her cookies into snow globes. The bases were red, while the globes were blue with white snow and an intricate white Christmas tree on each one. She'd spent practically her entire childhood perfecting the design with her grandmother. "Thank you."

Someone cleared their throat and said, "Excuse me, Ms. Mann?"

Olivia wiped her icing-covered fingers on her messy apron and turned her attention to the man. He was one of the senior production assistants and was always the one who came to find her when there was a location change for filming. She wondered what area of the inn they wanted to take over tonight.

"Uh, hi. It's Marvin, right?" She held out a hand and then thought better of it. "Sorry. I think they might be a little sticky. What can I do for you?"

"We need to know it you'll approve a set design change for us. The director wants the outbuilding to be red instead of yellow. Follow me. I'll show you which one."

Olivia glanced back at Declan and said, "I'll be back as soon as I can."

Marvin led her outside and around to the back of the inn, pointing to the yellow potting shed. Anyone with eyes could see the peeling paint and know it needed a lot of love. She'd been planning to paint it in the spring, but just hadn't settled on a color yet.

"Do you mind if we paint it? The director is asking for the color red."

"No, not at all." Why would she care? She should be thanking them, after all. They were saving her from doing it herself or paying someone else to do it. This just saved her time and money.

"We can paint it yellow again after—" he started.

"Nope. I like red. Go ahead and paint it. Consider me grateful," she reassured him.

"Perfect. Thank you, Ms. Mann," he said before walking off to consult the powers that be.

Olivia made her way back to the kitchen to help Declan clean up their mess, but when she got there, she stood frozen in the doorway when she spotted Priscilla holding one of her snow globe-shaped cookies.

"This is the one. It's perfect," Priscilla said. "The recipe isn't too complicated, and it's gorgeous. Think of how these will look in print." She was practically giddy with delight.

"Um, Priscilla, those weren't the ones we made for you to choose from," Declan said, clearly trying to handle the actress with kid gloves. "Don't you think you'd be better off with one of the more advanced recipes? I think you'd be more likely to win."

"Nonsense." She waved a perfectly manicured hand. "No one is expecting me to be Martha Stewart. That's not my brand. But this? Simple and elegant. That they'll believe.

Great job, Declan. I really appreciate this. I'll just need you to show me how you did these decorations."

"Olivia—" he started, but the inn owner cut him off.

"I'm right here," she said, striding in with a forced smile. "I see you made your choice. The snow globes are pretty, right?"

"Very." For the first time in maybe ever, Priscilla smiled warmly at Olivia. "I don't know what it is about Declan here, but he just seems to be on the same page as I am. Like kindred spirits or something."

Olivia's stomach turned, and she wondered if she was going to vomit. Who was this woman, and what had she done with the surly actress who was never afraid to make a snide comment?

"Can you show me how to do this tomorrow after our coffee date?" Priscilla asked him.

"Um, sure," he said, sounding anything but certain as his eyes stayed trained on Olivia.

"Perfect. It's a plan." Priscilla placed her hand on Declan's shoulder as she walked by and trailed it across his back as she passed him.

Olivia forced herself not to say one word until the woman was gone. When she heard Priscilla's footsteps on the stairs, she finally walked over to Declan and took a seat on the stool beside him.

"I'm sorry, Olivia. I tried to tell her those were your cookies, but then you stepped in and..." He shrugged, looking miserable.

"It's fine," Olivia said with a sigh. "We never should've chosen the harder cookies anyway. If she hadn't seen mine, she probably would've demanded we give her three more samples. Don't worry about it. They're just cookies."

"The ones you made with your grandmother when you were a kid," Declan said.

"It wasn't grandma's secret recipe or anything," Olivia said, knowing that was hardly the point. "I'll just make something else. Maybe I'll do the marshmallow caramel ones and beat the pants off her."

"They are delicious," Declan said.

"Come on. Let's clean up and put these out for the crew." She made sure her tone was light when she added, "And while we're doing that, you can tell me all about your coffee date tomorrow morning."

Declan winced. "I ran into her this morning and we talked a little bit. She seems… I don't know, reflective? Sort of sad, but also resigned. Different than usual."

"Reflective?" Olivia asked. "Are you sure?"

"Yeah. She was talking about her childhood, and how her parents just wanted to use her to further their careers. She doesn't talk to them anymore. Honestly, I have no idea why she told me any of that. She just did and then after she was done, she asked if we could talk again. I didn't really think I could say no."

Olivia stared at him in disbelief. "What did she say about her parents?"

He frowned, studying her. "Basically that they didn't care about her and now she doesn't talk to them. Why?"

"I…" Olivia pressed a hand to her throat as the vivid memory of her dream came flooding back. Was it possible that Olivia had entered one of Priscilla's dreams? Was that why Priscilla was talking about her parents this morning?

"Olivia?" Declan asked. "Are you all right?"

"Yeah. Sorry. I just had a really weird dream last night about Priscilla and her parents. They were awful to her. So it's super weird that she was talking about that out of the blue."

Declan raised both eyebrows. "That's... something."

She nodded. "Definitely something."

CHAPTER 18

*D*eclan walked softly into his sister's house, knowing that when she heard him he'd be peppered with a million questions. All of them about where he'd been the night before and with whom. But he wouldn't have to answer. She'd know already.

He slipped through the kitchen and into the hall that led to his room. But before he could hide away, Payton appeared in the hallway, balancing on her crutches.

She didn't say anything, just looked at him with one questioning eyebrow raised.

"Don't start." Declan leaned against his door frame.

"Start what?" she asked, putting on an air of innocence.

"Payton." Declan shook his head. "Don't act dumb."

"Why not? You're acting like a selfish teenager."

"Selfish teenager?" he parroted. "That's a little harsh, don't you think?"

Payton glanced down at her leg that was still in a cast

and waved one of her crutches. "Not really. You're willing to let me stand here in the hallway to argue with you instead of insisting that I sit down. You also didn't call to tell me you wouldn't be home last night, so here I was wondering what the hell happened to you. I mean, it's not like you have a curfew, but a text would've been nice. All you had to do was answer the one I sent. Hell, at this point, I would've taken a smoke signal. If it hadn't been for a text from Olivia earlier, confirming that you were indeed at work this morning, I'd still be wondering if you'd slid off the side of the mountain."

"Son of a..." Declan strode over to her, took the crutches from her, and then picked her up in his arms and carried her to the living room where he set her down gently on the couch so she could prop up her foot.

"That wasn't exactly the response I was looking for," she said dryly. "I could've crutched my way in here, you know."

"Yes, I do know," he said as he disappeared back into the hall and retrieved her crutches for when she wanted to get up again. "Do you need anything? Water? Tea? I could cook you dinner."

"Dinner would be nice," she said, still sounding salty. "Last night I had cold Pop-Tarts."

Declan came to a sudden stop. "You did?"

"Yep. My leg was aching and standing around long enough to make anything wasn't gonna happen. So I just grabbed the closest thing."

"You should've called me. I'd have brought you dinner," he said.

Payton laughed. "Seriously? You didn't even text me back so I wouldn't worry."

"Pay…"

"Nope. I can take care of myself. If I really needed something else, I could've ordered something and had Lemon Pepperson deliver it. Christmas Grove isn't quite the small backward town you think it is. We might not have the commercial delivery places here, but we have community and we all help each other out."

He gave her a flat stare and then finally shook his head. "I'm sorry I acted like an idiot teenager last night. I promise to let you know when I'm not coming home so that you won't worry."

Her lips curved into a satisfied smile. "Thank you. Now was that so hard?"

He rolled his eyes but then cracked a smile when he said, "Don't push it, little sis."

"Tormenting you is just about my only form of entertainment these days, so suck it up."

"Noted." He retreated to her kitchen and after quickly scanning her fridge and cupboards, he got to work.

Once dinner was ready, he got her a glass of iced tea, made up her tray, and carried it into the living room. "I hope you're in the mood for a smothered burrito. I would've made you a margarita, but I'm guessing that's not a great idea with your pain meds."

Payton grinned at him. "Best brother in the world."

"Only brother, but I'll take it." He handed her the tray and then sat across from her on one of the armchairs.

"You're not eating?" she asked even as she cut into the

burrito.

"I'm headed back to the inn. I'll eat there."

"Are you staying the night?" she asked, clearly trying to keep her tone light.

But Declan could see right through her. She was worried and trying not to let it show. But who was she worried about, him or Olivia? "Probably. I'll be sure to text you and let you know for sure this time. What can I say? I've lived alone for a long time now. I'm not used to checking in with anyone."

She put her fork down. "I'm not trying to keep tabs on you, Declan. You know that, right? I just don't want to worry."

"I know. I should've thought of that." He leaned forward, clasping his hands together. "This isn't really what you want to talk about, though, is it?"

"No, not exactly." She sighed. "I feel like the annoying parent or something. You're not going to start hiding out in your room and never telling me anything again, are you?"

He ran a hand through his sandy blond hair and snorted softly. "I guess it depends on how this conversation goes."

Payton's lips twitched as she let out an amused huff. "That's fair. You already know what I'm going to say though, don't you? I just don't want to see either you or Olivia get hurt."

"We don't want that either, Pay. We aren't going into this blindly. We both know how it's going to end up. When you're better and it's time for me to leave, that will be the end of it. We're both okay with it. What's wrong with enjoying each other while we can?"

"Nothing. Nothing at all, Declan. But what about the fact that you're in love with her? How are you going to feel when you have to give her up?"

Declan felt a muscle in his neck twitch. This wasn't the conversation he wanted to be having. He'd expected her to warn him about hurting Olivia. He hadn't expected her to… to what? Call him out? Tell the truth? Make him face reality? Declan held his sister's gaze steady when he said, "I guess I'm just going to have to deal with it. You and I both know I can't stay here. Small towns don't work for me. Eventually I'd leave for a job in a city. I always do. It's my life. My choices."

"It is," she said, nodding her head. "It's your life, and I support whatever is best for you. You know that. But can you do me a favor?"

He'd do anything for her; she knew that. "What?"

"Take some time to really understand why you're always running. Is it from small towns or from something else?"

Declan ground his teeth together. That was one thing he didn't need to think about. He already knew exactly why he always left. But it was no one's business but his. "I'll do that, sis. Anything else?"

Payton frowned and gave him a worried look but shook her head. She'd said what she felt she needed to say. "Tell Olivia hello for me."

"I will." Declan stood and gave her a kiss on her forehead before heading for his room to grab a change of clothes.

When he was on his way out the door, his sister called out, "Love you! The burrito is delicious."

"Love you, too," he called back and slipped out the door.

CHAPTER 19

*O*livia tapped the keys on the computer at the registration desk as she listened to the guest on the other end of the line. They were booking an entire year in advance in order to celebrate their first anniversary in Christmas Grove.

"That's wonderful," Olivia said into the phone. "Your wedding is Christmas Eve? That sounds lovely." She finished taking the reservation, congratulated the bride and groom, and told them she couldn't wait to see them next year. Just as she was replacing the phone receiver, she heard a huff of irritation and glanced up to see Priscilla standing there with her hands on her hips.

"Ms. Cain, is there something I can do for you?" Olivia asked her.

The actress slammed a remote down onto the counter. "You can explain why the batteries are missing out of this remote."

Olivia glanced at the remote and then back at Priscilla and frowned. "I'm sorry. The batteries are missing?"

"Was I unclear? Do I really need to repeat myself? I used this remote yesterday. This evening when I went to turn on the television it failed. I considered calling to have someone else deal with it, but after dealing with people all day, I'm sure you can understand that I just didn't have the energy. So I checked the battery compartment and found it empty. I would like you to figure out who did this and fire them. But first, I'd like a fresh set of batteries so that I can go relax after my long day of working."

No batteries? Why would anyone take the batteries from the remote? Olivia had two different employees who serviced the rooms. She'd check with them immediately after she dealt with Priscilla. After picking up the remote and confirming that it didn't have any batteries, Olivia looked up at Priscilla and said, "My deepest apologies. I will get to the bottom of this as soon as possible. Give me just one moment and I'll have new batteries for you."

"Fine." Priscilla turned around to face the magical tree and crossed her arms over her chest.

Considering how Priscilla had so often blown her top, Olivia was impressed with how restrained she was managing to be. If someone had stolen the batteries out of Olivia's remote, she'd probably be less rational. Maybe because it was such a petty thing to do. She rummaged around in the desk, found a fresh pack of batteries, and then replaced them in the remote.

"Here you go, Ms. Cain." When Priscilla turned to get the

remote, Olivia continued. "I am very sorry about this. Please know that I consider this completely unacceptable behavior and it will be dealt with promptly."

"This is the second incident today. I want my room made off limits to any of your staff."

Olivia raised her eyebrows. "You don't want us to come in and clean daily?"

"Oh no, that's not what I said at all. I don't want any of your staff in there, but I didn't say anything about you. Each day while I'm working, I want you to freshen my room. And while you're there, you can take Tater and Scooter out for a short walk. They're getting a little fluffy around the middle from all the non-activity."

Before Olivia could form a response, Priscilla swept up the stairs, her head held high and her shoulders back as if she were royalty.

"She's angry. Serves her right." Lizzie said as she popped into existence right next to Olivia.

Olivia turned to her. "What do you know about this?"

"Who me?" The ghost pointed at herself, feigning innocence. "I don't know anything. I'm just a ghost that roams the halls."

"And my apartment, which leads me to believe you have access to the rooms, too. Who did this?"

Lizzie grinned.

Olivia groaned. "And the mayo shampoo? Was that you, too?"

"Is it my fault that the packets were left out after sandwich night?"

"You do realize you're making my life miserable because of these antics, right?" Olivia scrubbed her face with both hands. "Now I have to clean her room and walk her dogs. If there is one thing that Priscilla Cain excels at, it's figuring out when to ask for unreasonable things that no one can object to. How was I supposed to say no when someone has been sabotaging her room?"

Lizzie grimaced but then perked up. "Did you say walk her dogs? That's not terrible, right? They're really cutie pies."

"They are," Olivia said with a sigh. "The truth is I don't mind walking her dogs. I'd do that willingly anyway. It's the fact that I now look like an incompetent inn owner. Sabotaging someone's room is just so uncool, Lizzie."

"Hey, I have to get my kicks somewhere. It hasn't been a picnic being dead all these years." She waved her fingers at Olivia, clearly not at all remorseful, and then slowly faded back into the ether.

"As if I don't have enough trouble," Olivia grumbled to herself.

"Do I dare ask?" Declan asked from behind her.

She turned her attention to him and instantly felt better. Why was that? He hadn't done anything to compensate for a mischievous ghost who didn't care one ounce how much trouble she caused. "On top of everything else, I'm now Priscilla's personal maid and dog walker."

"What?" Declan looked horrified.

She filled him in on Lizzie the ghost's antics and how she'd been roped into the extra duties.

Instead of trying to tell her how to fix the problem,

Declan just opened his arms and invited her in for a hug. Olivia went willingly. He wrapped his arms around her and held her close, just comforting her for as long as she needed. "You know, if Paul were here, he'd have already tried to come up with five different solutions to my problems. And I can guarantee they'd have all made the problem worse."

"He was clearly an idiot," Declan said. "Anyone with eyes can see you can handle it. And that if you need help, you'll ask."

She pulled back to look up at him through watery eyes. "Why are you so good to me?"

"It just comes naturally, I guess." He brushed a lock of Olivia's hair out of her eyes and then added, "Are you done for the evening?'"

"Yes. Are you?"

He nodded.

"Good. Let's go say hi to Apollo," she said, taking his hand and leading him to her apartment.

"How did you know that's why I was hanging around?" Declan teased.

"It's always about Apollo. I've just accepted it." She winked at him.

As soon as they were in her apartment, he spun her around, pressing her up against the door. "I've been waiting all day for this."

"Me, too."

Declan dipped his head and then took her mouth, showing her just how much he'd longed for her since he'd left her that morning.

"Woof. Woof." Apollo ran up and started rubbing his head against Olivia's leg.

When he flopped down at their feet and started rolling around with his paws in the air, Olivia started to laugh into the kiss.

Declan glanced down and chuckled. "Looks like what Apollo wants is what Apollo gets." He knelt down and rubbed the dog's belly, rewarding his clownish behavior.

"He has been on his own most of the day," Olivia said, sitting down on the floor right there to give her dog the attention he deserved. "He's only seen me for bathroom breaks."

Declan smiled at her as he continued to love on Apollo. "You know what?"

"What's that?" she asked, her eyes sparkling and her cheeks flushed.

"The moment you walked in here, all the tension of your day just seemed to disappear," he said, sounding shocked.

"It's kind of weird, right? That never used to happen at the farm." Olivia leaned down and kissed Apollo's head. "But here? I dunno. I guess it's because I love the inn. I love Christmas Grove. And when I'm in here, done with work, I just enjoy what I have." She looked lovingly down at her dog. "Apollo helps, too."

"I bet he does." Declan gazed at her for a long moment. Then he stood and held his hand out to her. "Let me give you one more thing to love."

A tingle started low in Olivia's belly, and as she got to her feet, her entire world narrowed to Declan. She brushed her lips over his cheek and whispered, "Just as long as it's you."

He tightened his grip on her hand and then led her into the bedroom where she could have him all to herself for a few hours.

CHAPTER 20

"*What are we doing here?*" *Olivia asked Priscilla. They were standing outside a large two-story house that was on a high bank overlooking a large body of blue water.*

"*I wanted to see what I was missing,*" *the actress said.*

Olivia watched her, noting her sad expression as she stared at the front door. "*Are we going in?*"

"*I'm not sure I can.*" *Priscilla turned to leave, but then a car came up the drive and she froze, clearly waiting to see who was in the car.*

Olivia squinted, trying to see through the windshield, but the sun was too bright and it nearly blinded her. It wasn't until the man stepped out of the vehicle that she recognized him.

"*Leo? What's he doing here?*" *Olivia asked.*

"*It's his parents' home,*" *Priscilla said.* "*He's here in Befana Bay for Christmas.*"

"*Christmas in Befana Bay?*" Olivia glanced around at the clear blue skies. "*Are we in Washington?*"

"*Yep. That land mass over there is the Olympic Peninsula.*" She pointed across the Hood Canal to the west. "*Leo West grew up here. Did you know that?*"

"*No.*"

Priscilla was quiet as she watched Leo extract his bags from the trunk of his car.

"*He can't see us, can he?*" Olivia asked.

Priscilla shook her head.

"*Interesting,*" Olivia said.

"*What's interesting?*" Priscilla asked with a frown.

"*That we're having a dream about Leo instead of you. Last night was all about remembering your childhood Christmases. But this one? Looks like you weren't invited.*"

Priscilla snorted. "*Of course I was invited. How else do you think I knew he'd be here?*"

"*Leo invited you to Christmas?*" Olivia asked in pure shock. *She knew the two were friendly, but she'd had no idea they were close enough to invite each other for a major holiday.*

An elegant woman of about seventy strolled out onto the porch. "*Leo, you're here!*"

"*I'm here, Mom,*" he said cheerfully. "*With plenty of time to deck the halls and trim the tree.*"

"*If you think we didn't already do that, then you haven't been paying attention to how excited your nona is to meet this lovely girl of yours.*" *His mother hurried down the steps and made a beeline for the car.*

"*Mom!*" Leo called. "*Priscilla's not here. We broke up.*"

Olivia turned to the actress in shock. "*You were dating Leo?*"

"I was. Now I'm not."

Everything went black for just a second, and then suddenly Priscilla and Olivia were transported into the house and were standing behind the couch while they watched Leo pace along the floor-to-ceiling windows that looked out over the water.

"Leo, why are you so agitated?" asked a man who looked a lot like Leo, only he was taller and thinner. "Priscilla never comes for Christmas. She never comes here period. Why are you so worked up this year?"

"She came here with me in the summer last year," Leo said with a frown. "She loved it."

"I really did," Priscilla told Olivia. "The summers here are lovely. Leo is lovely when he's here, too. It's obvious he's content here."

Olivia stopped paying any attention to Leo. She was far too interested in studying Priscilla's face as she talked about Leo West. Her features softened, and there was a lightness to her tone that hadn't been there before. If Olivia was a gambling woman, she'd have bet fifty bucks that Priscilla considered Leo the love of her life.

The only time her expression faltered was when Leo said, "It's over, man. This time it's really over."

"Why now?" his slimmer look-alike asked. "You've been breaking up and making up for well over a decade. I'm sure it will be the same this year."

Leo shook his head, "Not this time, Nate. I told her if she canceled last minute this year I was done. I am so tired of always being second choice. To her career, to her secrets. I'm over it. I deserve to be a consideration in her life, and she's made it clear

I'm not. It's time I found someone else who can give me what I need."

"What's that, brother? What do you need?"

"Someone who isn't afraid of marriage. Who wants to settle down somewhere and live a normal life outside of Hollywood. At least sometimes, anyway. For a summer or the holidays. I need to recharge. Right now, I'm fairly certain being in LA all the time has turned me into a dick."

Olivia snickered. "Sometimes."

"It's an act, you know," Priscilla said. "The charm Leo unleashes on people is what he thinks people want to hear. This conversation Leo's having with his brother, it's the real Leo. He's hurt and vulnerable and sticking up for himself. It almost makes me want to change my mind and come here for Christmas."

"Will you?" Olivia asked.

"I seriously doubt it. I'm not that strong."

Leo's brother clapped him on the back and said, "Come on, brother. You need a distraction. Ready for a beer?"

"So ready, you have no idea."

The blackness creeped in again, and when Olivia reoriented herself, she was in a high-rise condo that appeared to look over New York City. Her companion Priscilla was gone, and the only one in the room was sitting in an armchair, wearing a robe and drinking champagne straight from the bottle.

"Priscilla?" Olivia called, trying to get her attention. But it was useless. Priscilla couldn't see her.

She took one more drink of the champagne before raising it in a toast. "Merry effing Christmas, Mom and Dad. Aren't you proud? You got what you wanted all along. A cold-hearted woman who has everything except the one thing she needed most. Love."

CHAPTER 21

*D*eclan reluctantly left a sleeping Olivia. She'd been restless for most of the night and had finally settled into a deep sleep. He didn't want to disturb her. Instead, he took it upon himself to take Apollo out, feed him, and then put the pup back to bed with his mom. After giving her a whisper of a kiss on the cheek, he slipped out and went into the kitchen to put the coffee on.

His sister's words from the night before kept haunting him.

What exactly was he running from? Olivia? Commitment? Or was it actually about being trapped in a small town?

His head told him there wasn't anything here in Christmas Grove to run from. There didn't seem to be a gossip mill like what he'd been used to back home. Besides, he wasn't a kid anymore. Did he really care what other people said about him?

The answer was a resounding no.

So what was it then?

"You're thinking a little too hard for this early in the morning," Priscilla said.

Declan turned and found the actress standing just inside the kitchen. "Would you ever live in a small town?" he blurted.

She raised one eyebrow. "I am right now and will be for the next couple of months. Why?"

"I meant full time. Could you make a place like Christmas Grove your forever home?" he pressed, not at all sure why it mattered what Priscilla Cain would do.

"Not in Christmas Grove," she hedged. "It's a little too sweet for me. But there *is* a small town in Washington that's really appealing. My issue is that it's far too removed from Hollywood. A move like that would really limit my opportunities. It's not just auditioning for a role. It's the networking that keeps me top of mind for producers looking to get stars attached to a project."

"So you would if it didn't hurt your career?" he asked curiously.

"I like to think so." There was sadness in her expressive eyes, and Declan wondered if he'd hit a nerve. "Is there coffee?"

"Yes, of course." Declan shook himself, trying to put his thoughts out of his mind. He wasn't going to find the answer talking to Priscilla Cain. The woman wasn't exactly the picture of happiness. If anything, she looked miserable. He handed her a cup of coffee and asked, "Rough night?"

"I didn't sleep well," she said and gratefully took the coffee. "Too much on my mind."

"About the movie?" he asked.

"Nah. It's going fine. In fact, we might even be wrapping early. It seems because we filmed in a place that already has snow, production has been going a lot faster." She rolled her eyes. "This is personal. I think I might be at the point where I need to make some really hard life choices and honestly, I'm a little terrified."

"Want to talk about it?"

She shook her head. "No. A thousand times no. What I want to do is learn to decorate those cookies so I don't look like a fool later this week when we do *The Great Christmas Grove Cookie Bakeoff.*"

Just when Declan thought she might have been becoming a decent human, she went and ordered him to teach her Olivia's cookies. He knew that's what Olivia wanted him to do, so he downed the rest of his coffee and got the kitchen set up. After handing Priscilla an apron, he pointed to the mixing bowl. "It's time to make icing."

Priscilla did a lot of complaining about how much work it all was. It wasn't. Making icing was the easiest thing to do. It was just that they had to make multiple batches for all the different colors.

"Why can't I have this ready when I go to the show?"

"You mean why can't I have it ready for you," he corrected.

She gave him a sheepish smile. "You know what?"

He stared at her, waiting for her to answer.

"There's only one other person in my life who tells me when I'm being an ass. I find it... refreshing."

"You should hold on tightly to whoever that is. Having someone who will tell you the truth is a gift," he said, realizing that Olivia was that person for him. Sure, Payton did too, but that wasn't the same. She was his sister; she was supposed to annoy him. He'd never dated anyone who was as honest and straightforward as Olivia. He was going to miss that when he left Christmas Grove.

That annoying voice in his head said, *you don't need to go.*

Declan sucked in a sharp breath, drawing Priscilla's attention.

"Something wrong?" she asked.

"Nope." He stood to position himself in front of the cookies. "We should get started."

"Sure. I've got a scene this afternoon, so the sooner we do this, the better." She stood beside him with her hands in her pockets.

Declan refrained from rolling his eyes and handed her a piping bag. "Fill this with the red icing."

Priscilla looked at it like he'd just handed her a complex math equation that she had no hope of solving.

Declan, patient as ever, filled his piping bag to show her how it was done. "See, easy, right?"

Priscilla looked pointedly at Declan's hands and said, "If I get red dye on my hands, it's going to ruin the shot. It's the proposal scene today."

She had to be messing with him, right? No, she wasn't, and Declan knew he shouldn't be surprised. Priscilla Cain was the walking definition of entitled, and the only reason she was getting away with so much while staying at The Enchanted was because Olivia needed this contract in order to stay afloat over the winter. He doubted Priscilla knew anything about Olivia's situation, but it still rankled that the actress gladly took advantage of any opening to make things difficult for her.

In an effort to speed up their time in the kitchen together, Declan filled her piping bags for her and then showed her how to make the decorations on the cookies.

"Those don't look like the ones from yesterday," Priscilla said, frowning at the cookie he'd just finished.

"Yes, it does. Red base, blue sky, mound of snow, and a Christmas tree. What did you think it was supposed to look like?"

"Neater. More precise. That's what I liked about them. These that you just showed me? They're sloppy."

Declan carefully laid his piping bag down on the kitchen counter and said, "That's because Olivia decorated the ones you saw yesterday. She's been doing it since she was a little kid with her grandmother. She was going to enter these cookies, but then you showed up and claimed them. And because she's willing to do just about anything to make her guests happy, especially you, she wouldn't let me say anything. So no, Priscilla, they aren't as neat as Olivia's. They couldn't be. I haven't spent decades honing my skills. You'll have to forgive me if I'm a subpar teacher."

"These were Olivia's?" Priscilla asked. "And you let me choose them anyway?"

"Yes, they're Olivia's, and no, I didn't let you do anything. Olivia did. I was just about to tell you they were off limits when she showed up and made it clear they weren't. But I very much doubt she'll be happy about you going on national television and claiming they're yours. Imagine having a memory like that with your grandparent co-opted by some rich famous person so she can garner even more attention."

"That's not—" Priscilla started but then shook her head. "No, you're spot on." She sat heavily on her chair and stared helplessly at Declan. "You're right, I can't use these. But the reason I didn't pick the others is because I'd have made a fool of myself trying to make them, which is exactly why you chose those recipes for me."

"We didn't—"

She laughed. "Of course you did. I would have done the same thing in your shoes. It's the perfect revenge."

Declan's lips twitched, but he admitted nothing.

"You know, I had a grandmother who was kind to me, too. She made shortbread cookies. Any chance you can teach me how to do that? I think Olivia's onto something. There isn't a single other relative in my life that I'd like to honor, but my grandmother? Yeah, she was special."

This time Declan gave her a full-blown smile. "That sounds like a lovely idea, Priscilla. And as a bonus, shortbread cookies are really simple. You should be able to master them in no time."

The actress's eyes lit up. "Okay, let's do this."

Declan quickly cleared the icing and sugar cookies so that they could get started.

Forty-five minutes later, they were in the process of cleaning up when a deep chuckle came from the doorway.

"What is this I see?" Leo asked. "Priscilla Cain doing dishes? What in the world happened? Did you piss off the director again? Is this your punishment for annoying him to distraction?"

Priscilla stared at him coolly. "It's not a punishment, Leo. Declan was helping me learn to make cookies, and I'm just doing my part to clean up."

"Declan taught you to make cookies? What are you doing, Priscilla? Is he my replacement now that I'm done playing your game?" He turned his attention to Declan. "Word of warning, buddy. She's incapable of honesty. If you value that in a partner, stay the hell away from Priscilla Cain."

Priscilla winced as he stalked off.

Declan put a hand on her shoulder for support. "He's a jerk."

"He's right, though," she said, her eyes glassy. "I haven't been honest with him. I haven't even been honest with myself." She took off the apron, carefully folded it up, and set it on the counter. "Thank you, Declan. I'll make the shortbread cookies. Tell Olivia I'm sorry and that I'll be disappointed if she doesn't present her beauties at the bakeoff."

"I'll be happy to," Declan said as he watched her walk out of his kitchen.

CHAPTER 22

*O*livia stood on the back porch with three dogs milling around at her feet and reveled in the moment. It was a clear morning with a beautiful blanket of snow covering the ground. It was moments like these that gave her the desire to pinch herself.

A year ago, when she'd come home with her heart and her pride crushed, this dream of hers had seemed nearly impossible. Now she owned the inn, most of the money from the movie contract had just been paid to her that morning, and she could stop worrying so much about how she was going to survive while she built her business.

It had been a surprise when the check from accounting was handed to her. She'd just gotten to her desk when one of the producers came to see her and told her they were wrapping the film before Christmas. She was being paid her full fee and they'd be out of her hair within the week. The final payment would come after New Year's once the bookkeeper was back in the office.

It meant that Olivia would be lonely around the inn for the month of January since she didn't have any reservations booked, but she'd use that time to complete small projects and work on her advertising plan.

The downside, though, was Declan. Without any guests to cook for, she didn't really need him. He'd be free to go if he wanted.

Her heart started to ache at the thought, but she'd always known that their time together would be short. She just hadn't expected it to be *that* short.

The three dogs had all done their business and were now just sitting at her feet, waiting for her to do something. She should probably take them back inside, but she just wasn't ready yet. She wanted to enjoy the stillness of the morning. That feeling she got that made her feel like anything was possible.

She closed her eyes, breathed in deeply, and then let it out slowly, really trying to be present in the moment.

"It's not yoga class," Leo said, his tone far too snarky for Olivia's liking.

"Why are you here, Leo?" she asked without looking at him. "Don't you have a makeup chair you need to occupy?"

"Actually, no. I came out here looking for you," he said, all traces of his snark gone. "Can I talk to you for a minute?"

"Sure." She tugged on the dogs' leashes and the four of them moved toward the chairs on the covered patio. Olivia sat and gestured for Leo to join her.

Once he was seated, he said, "I'm thinking of giving up acting."

"Oh. Okay." She frowned. Why was he telling her this? "But not before the movie is done, right?"

"What? No, of course not. It'll wrap in a few days anyway. Did you know that finishing a movie earlier than scheduled is completely unheard of in our industry?"

"I'd heard rumors," she said with a chuckle. "I guess the producers and everyone else on down wanted to get home for Christmas."

"Everyone except one person." He averted his gaze. "That's the reason I wanted to talk to you."

Olivia stared at him, confused. "Um, okay. You want me to help someone be excited about going home?"

"No. That's not..." He shook his head. "There's no helping her. Trust me, I've tried everything. What I want to know is how you found the courage to leave your husband after so many years of trying to make it work."

Oh. That was a much deeper question than she'd imagined out of him.

"I take it you're in the middle of breaking up with someone?" She asked the question but felt she already knew the answer. After the heartbreaking dream she'd had the night before, she was certain that whatever Leo and Priscilla's relationship had been in the past, it was about to change forever.

"You could say that. I told her if she bailed on me and my family for the holidays again, then it's over. I just can't take it anymore. Holidays are for celebrating with family. But it's not just about that. It's been years, and she still can't seem to fully commit. So for my own sanity, I just need to move on. I was hoping you could give me some advice on how to do that."

Whoa. This man was looking for some sort of magical elixir that just didn't exist. Well, maybe it did, but it'd be dark magic and likely very dangerous, so she just ignored that bit of information and said, "You just have to do what is right for you. The one thing I learned through my divorce is that I have to make myself happy first. I can't live my life to make someone else happy. I just ended up resenting both of us."

"Leaving is what made you happy?" He was staring at her as if she had all the answers.

"I mean, I guess?" How could she explain this to help him understand? "My ex and I were on completely different trajectories for what we wanted out of life. We married young, and at least in my case, I didn't really know what I wanted until I realized I was never going to get it. So, after years of trying to make it work, I finally was kind to myself and left. It was the best decision for both of us. Just this morning as I was standing out here with the dogs, I felt more peaceful than I had the entire ten years I was married to my ex. Life, for me, is just better without him."

"So I should cut ties. It sounds like you're saying I should walk away," he said, staring at her earnestly.

"I didn't say that, Leo. I said I had to make the right decision for me. One that meant I wasn't sacrificing my emotional needs for someone else. If we'd had the same vision for our lives together, then I think I could've stayed and we'd have worked it out. But it was clear that was never going to happen. I think you need to talk to Priscilla. Have an open conversation about where your relationship is and what you both need from it and then decide."

"How did you know?" he asked, his voice so low that Olivia almost didn't hear him. "Did she tell you? Did you see us?"

Oops! She hadn't meant to say Priscilla's name. It'd just slipped out. She felt like she had a front row seat to their problems since she'd just dreamed about them the night before. A dream she was certain she'd shared with Priscilla. "No, she didn't. I just... assumed. Sorry. I didn't mean to pry."

He sat back in his chair and closed his eyes. "I've been trying to move on from Priscilla Cain for years. It's why I've been flirting with you. There's just something about you that draws people in. Did you know that?"

"No." Olivia had no idea what the man was talking about. Prior to Declan, she'd had exactly three relationships in her lifetime. And one of those had been when she was a literal kid. The other one was more like a friends-with-benefits situation, though it didn't exactly feel like that. Her relationship with Declan was everything she'd dreamed of, except for the part where he was planning to leave. But Olivia knew what it was like to be stuck in a life she didn't want, and she'd never ask that of him. Her only choices were to stay away from him now or accept that their time was coming to a close and enjoy every moment she could with him.

"You do," he said, sounding more sincere than he had since she'd met him. "Trust me. I know you're with Declan and I shouldn't have been getting in the middle of that. And I definitely owe you an apology. I'm just trying to figure out what to do once I close the door on a future with my longtime costar."

"I imagine it's been hard to make a choice to break away when you're coworkers, too," Olivia said.

"It has. That's why I'm not renewing my contract for another season. I'm going to move home and start a production company."

"Seriously? That's a huge change for you," she said.

"It is, but I'm ready for it. Befana Bay is sort of like Christmas Grove, only it's not centered around Christmas. It's more a town that caters to witches. Downtown is a treasure trove for witches looking for unique brooms, fun potions, rare herbs, and there's even a studio for witches to learn spell-casting. If you're a witch, it's the place to be."

"I've heard of Befana Bay. Wasn't the town founded by a descendant of a woman who suffered and escaped the Salam Witch trials and then spent the rest of her life bringing toys and candy to children as a way to keep a hold on her humanity?"

He nodded, and a genuine smile claimed his handsome face. "Yes, that's the story. Willa Parker founded the town, and it was speculated that she carried on the tradition of delivering the toys and candy until her death. No one knows who does it now, but it still happens every January 6th, on Founder's Day."

"You sound like you really love it," Olivia observed.

"I do. I miss it and the simplicity of life there. It's why I want to start my production company there. It's the perfect setting for more heartwarming stories that mirror *Merry Me for Christmas.*"

Olivia reached out and squeezed his hand. "It sounds like you've found your purpose. I have never seen you look happier or sound more authentic than right this moment, Leo. Don't ignore how you're feeling right now. If you don't follow your dreams because you put someone else first who won't do the same for you, then you're only going to wind up resentful and likely flirting inappropriately with women who may or may not already be taken."

He laughed. "That's one of the things I really adore about you, Olivia. You're not afraid to speak your mind. Thank you." He stood, crouched down to say hello to the dogs and to give both Tater and Scooter kisses as if he'd done it a hundred times before, and then disappeared back inside.

Olivia glanced down at the dogs. All three of them were looking up at her with adoring eyes. "Yeah, okay. You earned your treats." She fished them out of her pocket and fed them to the ravenous beasts before they guilted her to death. Then she took them inside and got to work.

CHAPTER 23

"*N*eed some help?" Declan asked as he walked down the long driveway toward Olivia. She was standing on an A-frame ladder, fighting with a light cover on the lamppost she'd had installed at the entrance of her driveway so that guests would see the sign no matter how dark it happened to be.

"I think I've just about... there!" The cover popped free and Olivia pumped her fist in the air in triumph. "Did it all by myself."

"Well done. But I wish you'd have asked someone to come out here with you. At the very least they could've been a flagger to make sure no one ran you down while you were on that death trap."

She handed him the cover and gestured for him to give her a new light bulb that was sitting near the bottom of the ladder. "I parked my Outback strategically so that no one could run me down," she insisted.

"Maybe, but that doesn't mean you couldn't have fallen off this ladder, and no one would've been here to help you," he said.

"You're here now." She smiled down at him sweetly.

Declan was torn between being annoyed that she'd get on a ladder out by the main road without help and being amused at how pleased she was with herself. "I *am* here now. And I would have been here earlier if you'd just told me you were doing this."

"I didn't need your help, Declan. I have changed a lightbulb or two in my time. I'm a woman, but I'm not helpless."

Oh hell. Of course she'd see his concern that way. "This has nothing to do with your gender," he said. "But I understand why it sounded that way. I have a healthy fear of ladders, okay? I fell off one when I was ten and broke my arm. I never use one now unless there is someone there to spot me. It's just good practice."

Olivia tightened the lightbulb one last time and looked down at him with concern in her expression. "Did that really happen?"

"Yes, it did. Ask Payton about it sometime."

"I will," she said with a nod and then gestured for the cover. Once she had it back in place, she climbed down the ladder and stepped right in front of him. Without a word, she slipped her arms around his waist and hugged him for a long moment. "I'm sorry I scared you. Next time, if you're here, I'll make sure to bring you with me to change a light bulb."

"Thank you," he said with a short nod as he collapsed the

ladder for her and hauled it to her Outback. He peered in the vehicle and then at the ladder. "How did you get this in here?"

"Like this." She grabbed it and stuffed it through the back window at a diagonal, leaving the thing sticking out more than half way. "If we were leaving the property that wouldn't work, obviously. But I just needed to get it down here. Back to the garage it goes."

Declan stared at the ladder, slightly horrified. It looked like it was going to slide right out. But he had to give her credit for taking on tasks herself and getting them done. If it had been Payton, she wouldn't have bothered. She'd have written down a list and asked him to start working his way through them. She'd always done that even though they'd never really shared a house as adults. He'd come visit and she'd hand him a list.

He didn't mind. In fact, it was nice to feel useful. He figured it was just his brotherly debt. No doubt he owed her a hell of a lot more than a to-do list for whatever kind of torture he'd put her through as kids.

But when it came to Olivia, it occurred to him that there was something sexy about a woman wielding a screwdriver.

"What else can I help you with?" Declan asked Olivia.

She frowned. "I'd love that, but don't you have work to do in the kitchen?"

"Not today. It's the joy of planning ahead." He winked at her. "Now I'm at your beck and call for the afternoon."

Her lips curved into a slow smile. "Beck and call, huh? Does that mean you'll do anything I ask?"

"Most likely," he said, letting his gaze roam down her body as his imagination ran wild.

Olivia walked up to him and placed her palm on his chest as she leaned in and whispered, "My gutters need to be cleaned."

He sputtered with laughter. "I'm assuming you're not using the word *gutter* as a euphemism?"

"Unfortunately for you, no. I had them cleaned in the fall, but I noticed yesterday that there's a section on the back side of the house that they missed, and when it rains or snows, the water isn't draining the way it's supposed to. Would you mind taking a look at it? I mean, if you're not too scared of the ladder," she teased.

"Don't mock, Olivia," he admonished. "That's not nice. But if you think there's a chance you'll have dinner with me tonight, then I think I can do that for you."

"I'll do you one better," she said, looking up at him through lowered lashes. "How about a hot shower and I'll wash your back for you."

He didn't hesitate. "It's a deal. Now move over so I can secure this ladder. The last thing you need is for it to take out one of your trees on the way back to the inn."

She rolled her eyes but smiled as she gestured for him to help himself.

The pair spent the next few hours working together to take care of minor things around the inn. After the gutter was cleared, Declan helped her replace a loose board on her back porch. Then they cleared away some dead vegetation that the last snow had finally killed off. And finally, while Olivia was touching up a scuff on the front door that had appeared the day before after the crew was done filming, Declan hauled multiple bags of garbage left by the crew to the dump.

When he got back, Olivia was waiting for him on the porch, sipping a hot cup of coffee.

"Hey," he said, sitting next to her. "All done?"

"For today. I was just enjoying the sunset before I go in and get cleaned up."

"Before *we* get cleaned up," he corrected.

Chuckling, she nodded. "Ah, yes. I didn't mean to imply that I was backing out of our deal."

"I didn't think you were," he said graciously, even though it had occurred to him that maybe she'd changed her mind. If she had, that would've been perfectly fine, but the thought of her hands running all over his body had been the one thing he'd thought about all day.

"I had an interesting talk with Leo West today. It was more of a counseling session than a chat, but it was still interesting," she said out of the blue.

"You did? When?" he asked.

"This morning while I was taking the dogs out."

"You mean while I was teaching Priscilla how to make cookies?" he asked, finding that a little ironic since he'd thought his time with Priscilla had been a little like a counseling session, too.

"Probably. He and Priscilla have been in a relationship on and off for years. Did you know that?"

"No, but I had my suspicions. Payton and I spotted them making out one day when we were in town."

"Interesting," she said. "Anyway, he's tired of waiting for

her and is moving to Washington and going to start an independent production company. So their show is likely to end."

"A lot of people will be disappointed," Declan said.

"Probably, but I understand why he's doing it. Waiting around for someone who's never going to give him what he needs is detrimental, so when he asked me what I thought, I told him he should do it."

For some reason, Declan's heart started to ache. "Just like that? He should up and go?"

"It's not 'just like that.' I get the feeling this has been in the making for literally years," she said, staring down at the wooden deck.

"Right." Why was Declan feeling so strange about this piece of information? Was it because Olivia had been so quick to tell Leo to give up on his relationship? What if Priscilla realized he was more important than whatever had been holding her back? What if this was the push she needed? "Priscilla decided not to use your cookies for the contest," he said, changing the subject.

"She did?" Olivia sounded surprised by the news. "Why? Were they too hard for her?"

He chuckled softly. "Yes, but I don't think that's the only reason. She took issue with the way I was decorating them. She said they weren't up to par, and when I told her that's because they were cookies you made and were planning to enter, she had a change of heart. She didn't understand why we didn't tell her, especially when she learned you used to make them with your grandmother. So she switched to shortbread cookies because it turns out she also had a grandmother she wants to honor."

Olivia sat next to him with her mouth hanging open in what appeared to be utter shock. Finally, she blinked. "No way."

"Way," he said, grinning at her. Damn, she was cute.

"That's really something," Olivia said. "Well, that makes me happy. I'm glad to hear that underneath all those walls she keeps around her, there is a real human lurking around. Maybe with time, she'll find a way to meet Leo halfway. I guess hope springs eternal." She winked at him

"Yeah, maybe so," Declan said almost to himself, wondering if the same could be said for him. Was he just like Priscilla? Creating walls so he didn't have to deal with the hard stuff? That was something he didn't want to contemplate. If it was true, he'd been lying to himself about what he really wanted for years.

Olivia stood and held her hand out to Declan. "Now, where are we with that shower?"

He glanced up at her, and his entire body started to ache with the need to be in her arms. Taking her hand, he stood and said, "I think it's the next thing on our to-do list."

She grinned. "I think so, too."

CHAPTER 24

"*You're back again,*" Priscilla said, sounding despondent in the evening twilight.

"*So are you,*" Olivia said as she stared up at a large brick mansion that was covered in overgrown ivy and looked a little like it belonged on the set of American Horror Story.

"*I don't have a choice.*" She walked up to the front door and opened it easily. "*You're the one who brings me here.*"

Olivia followed the actress and asked, "*What? I don't do that. I'm just dreaming. Ever heard of dreamwalking? I'm pretty sure that's what's happening here.*"

"*Whatever you want to call it. I never dream about my life unless you're here.*" She walked through a dark, arched hallway and into a large wood-paneled living room. The drapes were drawn and the only light came from a small lamp on an end table where an older woman with silver hair sat with a blanket over her legs and a brindle-colored shih tzu in her lap.

"Look at me," Priscilla said. "I just sit in that chair all day with my dog, waiting."

Olivia let out a small gasp. "That's you?" She moved so that she could get a good look at the older woman's face and knew it was true. It was definitely Priscilla. "It is you," Olivia whispered as if the older woman might hear them talking.

She didn't look feeble. She sat up straight and was wearing a stylish pantsuit with delicate jewelry. "What are you waiting for?"

"Not what, who." Priscilla gave Olivia a tight smile. "Leo, of course. Who else?"

"This version of you has been pining for him all these years?" Olivia asked.

"I doubt I pined in the beginning. There were still movies to be made. Life to be lived. But now... what else is there to do but sit and think about what might have been?"

"Oh, I don't know. Garden? Make new friends? Bake cookies?" Olivia said off the top of her head.

"Who's to say I don't do those things? Did you see what the date is?"

Olivia glanced around, searching for any clue as to what day it was, but then she spotted it on the phone sitting next to the older Priscilla. It was December 25th. Christmas day.

"I always wait for Leo to show up on Christmas. He always wants me to go home with him. I never do, and then he comes to find me on Christmas. But I don't think he's coming this year. I don't think he's come in many years."

Priscilla waved a hand toward a small pile of envelopes. They were all postmarked many years earlier from Befana Bay, WA. Leo's name was on the return address.

Olivia went and picked up the letter that was laying on top of the pile and started to read.

My dearest Priscilla,

Life with you over the past two decades has been both my greatest pleasure and my greatest heartbreak. I have waited for years to be able to call you my own, hoping that one day you'd see that there was more to this life than just making movies together or finding comfort in each other's flesh. You've been my best friend and confidant for so long I no longer remember what my life was like before you walked into it.

But unfortunately, I have never been your confidant. Not in the way that you've been mine. You've never opened all of yourself to me. There is a part you keep hidden, one that you don't show anyone, and I'm convinced you can't give it to anyone even if you wanted to. It's for this reason that I must say goodbye to you now.

It just hurts too much to know that I can't be for you what you are to me. It hurts too much knowing that we will never share that great love that we've acted out so many times in the films we've done together. If I thought there was even a chance there was hope for us, I'd never leave your side, but I must do this for me, and I must make the break now, or I never will.

I love you with all my heart and hope you find joy in the years to come,

Your Leo

"Oof. That's heartbreaking," Olivia said, wiping at her eyes.

"It's my own fault," Priscilla said. "I pushed him away. I

always made him come running, and eventually I lost the only person I ever loved."

She started to walk away, but Olivia grabbed her wrist and said, "It's not too late, you know. There's still time to change the trajectory of this path you've been on."

"How exactly am I supposed to do that? Do you see the date on that letter?"

Olivia glanced down at the yellowing parchment. Dec 21ˢᵗ, 2022. It would be written in just two days' time. "He's only going to write this because you refuse to go home with him for Christmas. You refuse to budge and are denying him a fulfilling and happy life by always making him chase after you! Don't you understand, Priscilla? This is your wakeup call. If you want to live a life with Leo, you have to meet him halfway. Find a way to make it work for both of you. If you can't, then you have to let him go for both of your sakes."

"I don't think I can," she said, staring at her older self.

"You'd rather have this life than one that includes family? A family that is nothing like the one you grew up with? They love each other, Priscilla. No one is using their child to get ahead. No one is working on Christmas day. They are celebrating each other. What about that makes you so afraid?"

"All of it." She wrapped a hand around her neck, clearly distressed. "I don't belong there."

Olivia grabbed Priscilla by both arms, stared her straight in the eye, and said, "You deserve love, Priscilla. You do. That little girl who's still inside of you and is desperate for a family, she does too. Do it for her. Do it for Leo. Do it for the woman in that chair. Most importantly, don't pass up on an opportunity to love because you're scared. You're far too resilient for that. If there is one thing Priscilla Cain isn't, it's a coward. Now act like it!"

Priscilla's eyes were wide with shock as she stared at Olivia, seemingly speechless.

Olivia cleared her throat and carefully released the other woman.

As soon as Olivia let go, the world went dark.

Olivia awoke with a start, her heart pounding and her skin damp with sweat. She stared up at the ceiling, trying to orient herself. Had she really dreamwalked into Priscilla Cain's dream and shouted at her to get her act together, or was Olivia just losing her mind?

She figured the chances were fifty-fifty at the moment.

Rolling over, Olivia found the bed empty. Declan was gone and so was Apollo. She glanced at the clock. It was just past eight. Later than she usually slept, but after that nightmare, she supposed she needed it. Declan must have gotten up to take Apollo out.

A girl could get used to that treatment.

"Yeah, we should get together to talk about that," Declan's voice floated in from the other room. "I've just started to think about the menu and what kind of atmosphere I want, so that's all up in the air."

There was silence, and then when Declan started talking again, his voice was muffled and Olivia couldn't make out what was being said. It didn't matter. She didn't want to hear it anyway. Plans about his restaurant just reinforced the fact that he'd be leaving soon.

She rolled over and groaned as she placed the pillow over her head. Hearing him talk about his restaurant just made it real, and she wondered if he'd leave sooner now that filming was done.

With a heavy heart, Olivia climbed out of bed and went to drown herself in her shower. At least while she was in there she wouldn't have to hear about menu options for Declan's fancy new Napa restaurant.

When she finally emerged from the bathroom forty-five minutes later, she was relieved to see that Declan was no longer on the phone. Instead, he was busy writing a checklist of things to do.

As soon as he saw her, he stood. "I've got to go run some errands. Do you want me to meet you down at the bakeoff studio? Will they let supporters in?"

Olivia didn't answer him at first. Instead, she pressed up onto her toes and gave him a lingering kiss that made him groan deep in his chest.

"Now that we have that out of the way," she said with a small smile, "we can start the day. Yes, I'd love it if you met me at the studio. No, I'm not sure they'll let you in. I'll text you when I get there and let you know." She tried to glance at the list he was holding, but he'd folded the paper and she couldn't see what he was going to pick up.

It was probably things for the new restaurant. He was probably headed to the restaurant supply place that was only twenty minutes out of town. She told herself it made sense to stock up while he was here. Now that he wasn't needed at the inn, he had time to do those things.

That didn't mean that Olivia had to like it. The truth was, she'd become too fond of having him around. If she had her way, he'd never leave and they'd spend the rest of their days working together to make The Enchanted a place no one would ever forget.

"Gotta go!" Declan said with a wave as he slipped out the door.

Apollo came running and started to bark right up until the door shut in his face. He turned and gave Olivia a WTF look.

'Me, too, buddy. Me, too."

CHAPTER 25

*O*livia slammed her borrowed truck into Park, grabbed her bag of supplies, and ran into the makeshift studio that they'd set up in the teaching studio right there on Main Street. She was late due to no fault of her own. When she'd gone out to her Outback earlier that day, it hadn't started. The engine wouldn't turn over at all. She'd had to call Zach to rush over and loan her a vehicle until she could get it fixed.

That hadn't been too much of a problem, but by the time he'd gotten there and she'd dropped him back off at the Christmas tree farm, she'd lost an entire hour.

There was a large crowd outside the studio, no doubt all of them waiting to get a glimpse of someone Important. Olivia had to push her way through the crush of people to get to the door, just to find someone who could let her in.

"Sorry," a bored security guard said. "They aren't allowing a studio audience."

"I'm not part of the audience. I'm a contestant." She dug around in her purse, looking for her ID. Before she could find it, the door opened and Mrs. Pottson, the owner of Love Potions, poked her head out, spotted Olivia, and then tugged her inside.

"Come on. Hurry. There's no time for hair and makeup," Mrs. Pottson said. "They're getting ready to start the bakeoff."

"I was supposed to be here for hair and makeup?" Olivia chirped as her voice squeaked. "Seriously?"

"You were supposed to get a letter. You didn't get it?" Mrs. Pottson asked, sounding concerned.

"I…" Olivia shook her head. "Things have been hectic at the inn with the filming and all. I'm sure it was just misplaced. It's fine. No one is going to be looking at me anyway."

Mrs. Pottson guided Olivia into the makeshift studio and positioned her in the last station that was right next to the furnace.

Olivia pulled her jacket and scarf off and wondered what they'd say if she stripped down to her bra. It was hotter than Hades in the studio. No one else seemed to be particularly warm though, so Olivia chalked it up to being late and figured she cool down once she settled in.

"Oh, good! I see our final contestant is here. Now we can get started," a woman dressed in an elf outfit at the front of the room called out. She opened her arms wide as if talking to a room full of people instead of five and shouted, "You all have two hours to complete your cookies. Not a minute more. All the ingredients you asked for are on the table. Be careful with your measurements as there aren't any backup ingredients if you make a mistake. The only rules are you have two hours. At the end of two hours, your cookies will be judged. On your mark, get set, go!"

The instant quiet did a lot to soothe Olivia's nerves. She took a long moment to survey her supplies and the tools she'd brought with her. Everything seemed to be accounted for, so she first went over to her portable oven and turned it on to her desired temperature.

Then she got busy mixing the dough for her sugar cookies.

Everything was going smoothly until she heard Priscilla mutter a curse under her breath. Olivia glanced up and saw she was holding up a glass bowl that was cracked. It must have happened in transport.

"Here," Olivia said, handing her an extra. "Use this."

Priscilla hesitated for just a minute and then gave Olivia a grateful smile as she took it.

Olivia heard the judges talking about how kind that was and that they wished all contestants were that generous, and then they launched into stories about how previous contestants had actually tried to sabotage each other.

There was no time for gossip though, and Olivia shut out their voices and focused on her dough. She'd had it sitting in the fridge and when she couldn't wait any longer, she grabbed it and got to work on rolling out and shaping her cookies. Unfortunately, due to the furnace being right next to her and the heat level in the building, the dough warmed too quickly and it became an utter disaster to shape them into anything that resembled a snow globe, so she just went with round orbs and placed them in the oven for eight minutes. She set her timer and got to work on the icing.

With all the different colors she needed to make, the time got away from her. And when it seemed like a lot longer than eight minutes had passed, she glanced at the timer and found it had gone off but she'd never heard it.

She started screaming on the inside and then just let out a disappointed sigh when she saw that the edges were burned. There was no saving the cookies. All she could do was take them out, let them cool, and then decorate them the best she could.

While everyone was furiously working, the host came around and asked questions. When she got to Olivia, she didn't even comment on the burned cookies. Instead, she immediately started asking about her relationship with Leo West.

"We've been hearing around town that our new owner of The Enchanted has struck up quite the relationship with the sexy Leo West. Is there anything you want to tell us about that, Olivia?"

Olivia blinked at her, completely taken off guard. "Um, no?"

"That doesn't sound very confident. Is there trouble in paradise?" the woman asked.

"There is no paradise," Olivia said, finally finding her voice. "Leo and I are just friends. We had lunch once, but that's all it was. Sorry I can't give you any more gossip." Olivia smiled nervously. Man, where did people get these ideas?

"When you say you're just friends, does that mean you and Leo hang out?" the host asked.

"Sometimes. While he was filming, Leo and I had coffee in the mornings and would chat about our days before we went our separate ways. It was all very innocent."

"Well, I can't say I'd complain about waking up with Leo West. You're a lucky girl, Olivia Mann."

"I guess so," she said and then wiped her sweaty forehead with her elbow. If Olivia didn't get out of there soon, she was going to drown in her own sweat.

The rest of the competition was relatively uneventful. The host kept her distance while Olivia did her best to decorate her orbs. In the end, they looked nice, but if anyone tried to eat one, they were going to risk cracking a tooth.

Once it was time for judging, they lined all the cookies up and had the contestants sit together in a row. Olivia found herself sitting right next to Priscilla, who, of course, looked like she'd just stepped out of a fashion magazine.

Olivia stifled a sigh and once again came to the conclusion that life just wasn't ever going to be fair.

"How'd you do?" Olivia asked her.

"Okay, I think. The cookies came out great, but I'm not sure the decorations are enough. All I did was dip part of them in chocolate. They taste good but are maybe a little lacking in the excitement factor."

"You did better than me," Olivia said.

"Yours look incredible," she said.

"I burned them, so they are ruined. But I did pretty them up."

"I'm sorry," Priscilla said, and it sounded like she might have actually meant it.

It made Olivia second guess if the dream the night before was real. Would Priscilla Cain be sitting here next to her pretending nothing happened if Olivia had dreamwalked her? Olivia didn't really think so, but she couldn't be sure.

"And the winner is... Priscilla Cain for the perfect holiday shortbread cookie!"

Olivia faded into the background, grateful that the competition was over. As she was packing up, Priscilla returned the glass bowl. And to Olivia's surprise, Priscilla wrapped her in a hug and whispered, "Thank you. For everything."

Then the movie star let go and hurried to the exit, disappearing before Olivia could say anything else.

But that's all it took. That one hug and those four words. The dreams were real, and Olivia had hope that everything would turn out the way it should with Priscilla and Leo.

CHAPTER 26

"What do you think?" Declan asked his sister as he paced her living room.

"About what?" Payton asked." You staying in Christmas Grove or you losing your mind and buying a restaurant without telling anyone?"

He cleared his throat and rubbed at the knot that was lodged in his chest. He'd signed the papers this morning and then came straight to his sister's house to share the news. "Both?"

She sat back in her chair and grinned at him. "First of all, I'd stand and give you a hug, but my foot aches, so we'll take a raincheck. Second, I'm thrilled you're staying in Christmas Grove. Have you told Matisse yet?"

Matisse was his boss, the owner of the Napa Valley restaurant. "Well, considering I couldn't have purchased the one here without his backing, I'd say he's not too upset about it. He did get me to try to run the Napa restaurant for a year while we build out Apollo's, but I declined. I can see his point, but I want to be here overseeing everything."

"I could help with that, you know. Or at least I can when my leg is better," Payton said.

"I know. It's not really about that, and I think we both know it," he said sheepishly.

Payton raised her hand, and when he walked over to her, she gave him a high five. "I'm proud of you, brother. But can I ask just one thing?"

"Sure," he said with a nervous chuckle. "Lay it on me."

"Did you discuss any of this with Olivia before you went through with buying her father's old restaurant?"

"No." He sat down heavily on the couch next to her chair.

"Why?" There wasn't any judgment in Payton's tone, just curiosity.

"Honestly, I wasn't sure I was going to go through with it." He leaned forward and rested his elbows on his knees. "I didn't want to disappoint her if I couldn't make myself commit."

"Declan, you know I love you, right?" she said.

He knew his sister was about to drop some hard truths. Normally it irritated him when she did that, but today, he thought maybe he needed to hear them. The last month had been a game-changer for him, but he still had a lot to learn if he was going to be in a relationship. "I know. Lay it on me."

"When you're in a relationship with someone, you have to trust them. That means telling them about the big and the little things in your life that are important to you. This kind of feels like something you should have discussed before you signed the paperwork. Especially since it was her family restaurant at one point."

Declan chewed on his bottom lip. He could see her point. But it wasn't like he was asking Olivia to go into business with him. He wasn't even asking her to move in with him. All he was doing was making plans to move to her town, to put down roots in Christmas Grove because it felt right. But it mostly felt right because of Olivia. She wasn't the only reason, but she was the biggest one. Finally he turned to Payton and said, "Point taken."

"Hey, I'm sure she'll be thrilled," Payton said, giving him an encouraging smile. "I just wanted to use that as a teaching moment. I'm sure you understand."

He laughed. His sister was the only one who could get away with that kind of stuff with him. And he wouldn't have it any other way. "Of course. Now onto the other important matters."

"Which are?"

"Whether or not you're going to work at the restaurant."

She frowned. "Work at the restaurant? But I have a job, and Olivia needs me." She scowled at her leg. "Or she will when I'm functional again."

"I know you have a job. I'm not trying to take you away from Olivia. But I do have to ask if you want to be a part of my restaurant. The family business. I'm not talking about you being the kitchen manager or breakfast chef or anything like that. What I want to know is if you would like to be a part owner?"

"Owner?" Payton's eyes widened so much he started to

wonder if they were going to pop right out of her head. "You want me to be part owner?"

"Why wouldn't I?" he asked, surprised that she was so surprised. "We're family. And you make the best damned sourdough bread I've ever tasted. It rivals any restaurant in San Francisco."

"Now you're just flattering me." She waved him off. "Stop telling me how wonderful I am and start talking details."

Declan had come prepared, and he pulled out a business plan for her to look at. "You can do as much or as little as you want. Your buy-in would cover a portion of the startup costs. You'd make money as an owner. If you want a job there, you'd also make that position's salary. We'd own eighty percent combined, and Matisse owns the other twenty percent. He'll be involved in financial decisions but will be mostly hands-off, just like he is with his other restaurants."

He watched as his sister's eyes got glassy with tears even as the grin on her face widened. She sniffed once and said, "Where do I sign?"

DECLAN FOUND Olivia perched behind her registration desk even though it was well past the time when she usually retreated to her apartment.

"Hey, stranger," he said, suddenly feeling uncertain of himself. Should he have called? It had been just this morning that he'd left her bed. But so much had happened.

He'd finalized the deal on her family restaurant. She'd filmed for *The Great Christmas Grove Bakeoff*, and although she had texted to say that they weren't allowing guests, he hadn't even seen the text until well after they'd finished. He felt incredibly disconnected and wasn't sure what to do about that.

Her eyes lit up when she saw him. But when she spoke, her words were forced. "Hey, stranger. How was the restaurant planning today?"

"You know about that?" he said, his heart racing. Who'd told her? Certainly not Payton. She'd only learned the news about an hour ago.

"Sure. I heard you on the phone this morning talking about menu ideas or something. I figured your errands had to do with the Napa restaurant." She tapped some keys on her computer, and when he glanced at the screen, he concluded she was updating the books.

"Oh. Yes. I was talking to Matisse, the owner of the Napa Valley restaurant. But, um, we weren't talking about that restaurant, we were talking about another one." He practically held his breath while he waited for her to acknowledge what he'd said.

She stopped typing and looked up at him. "Another restaurant? What does that mean? Are you no longer going to be moving to Napa?"

He nodded. "Yes, that's what that means, or at least I think that's what it means. A lot of it will depend on how you feel about it."

Olivia frowned. "How I feel about it? Why does that matter?"

He walked around the counter, took her hand in his, and then led her over to the chairs by the windows. The inn was quiet and he hadn't seen anyone around. No cars were in the parking lot and since filming wrapped, he had to conclude that everyone else had gone. If they weren't going to be interrupted, he thought this might be the perfect place to tell her since their friendship really did start over decorating her Christmas tree.

"Why all the buildup, Declan?" she asked. "You're making me nervous. Are you moving to Hong Kong or something? London? New York City? Paris even?"

"Would you come with me if I did?" he couldn't help asking her.

"That depends."

"On what?" he asked.

"Are we married in this highly unlikely scenario?" Her pointed stare nearly knocked him back a few feet.

"Um... Well, that's not really something I've thought about. But I guess if we're moving to Paris together, it's probably an option that is on the table."

"What about Apollo? Is he welcome?" She was still staring at him, studying him as if she were looking for something, but he had no idea what.

"Of course. We can't leave Apollo behind." That was a no-brainer. Marriage or no marriage, where ever they were, Apollo would be with them.

"Well, that's something, anyway." She sat back in her chair. "Where's the new restaurant, Declan? I need to find out if I need to apply for a passport."

His lips twitched. "You'd get a passport for me?"

Olivia pressed her lips together in a thin line and then glared at him. "If you're trying to annoy me, you're succeeding. I think I've already made it clear that if you leave the country, I'm at least going to want to visit you. If you wanted me to, anyway."

"Oh, I'd want you to," he said automatically. Then he took a deep breath and blurted out his news. "But lucky for us, it won't take an international airline ticket because the restaurant is going to be right here in Christmas Grove."

"What did you just say?" she demanded.

"I said—"

"You said Christmas Grove." She stood quickly. "You did, right? I'm not hearing things?"

He got to his feet, too. "No, you're not hearing things. It's right here in Christmas Grove, and unless you're fundamentally opposed to it, I'm going to stay here and run it."

She blinked rapidly, clearly holding back tears.

Declan moved into her space and wrapped his arms around her.

Olivia pressed her head to his chest and said, "I had a lot of questions, but right now I just want to enjoy this moment."

They stood in the lobby of her inn, the angels on the tree singing softly, the robins chirping, and the snowmen dancing, but in Declan's mind, there wasn't anything more magical than being in Olivia's arms.

CHAPTER 27

"*I* bought your father's restaurant," Declan said as he clutched a glass of wine.

Olivia was certain she'd heard him wrong. "Say that again?"

Declan put his wine glass down, leaned back into the couch, and petted Apollo, who was lying half in his lap. "Payton and I were out one day just driving around town when we came across your father's old building. At the time, I didn't even know that it was for sale. But for some reason, I just found it really intriguing and started to look into who owned it and what they might be doing with it, and then an idea started to form."

"The idea to buy it and stay in Christmas Grove? Even though you've told me numerous times that you're not a small-town guy and there was no way you'd live in a town like Christmas Grove? I think you might have even said something like that the first night we met."

"Yes. Even though I wholeheartedly believed that small-town living isn't for me, something has shifted in here." He pressed a finger to his chest. "It may have been pointed out to me that my steadfast excuse of not being cut out for small-town life might have been pure crap."

"Did Payton tell you that?" Olivia asked with a laugh. Leave it to her fiery friend to not mince words. It was one of the things Olivia loved most about her.

"She was one of them."

Olivia really wanted to ask who else had him thinking about things, but she really needed to get back to the topic of the restaurant. When he'd blurted the words, he'd left her speechless. "Why my dad's restaurant? Why not someone else's? There can't be a shortage of restaurant locations. They come and go all the time."

"Exactly. They do." He kept his gaze trained on her as he tried to be as honest as possible about his decision. "But the location of your dad's place is just special, overlooking the river like that. There is plenty of parking, and there's history there. I suspect the locals will all want to come out and see it. But both of those things are really just bonuses. What really got me is that it just feels right. Have you ever had that happen before? When you find yourself in a situation and you just know it was meant to be?"

Yes. With you. But there was no way she could tell him that. Not right now. It was too fast. Too soon to be making any kind of declaration like that. "I've been known to follow my gut a time or two. It's how I ended up with this place."

"Okay, then you understand at least somewhat." Declan picked up his wine glass and downed it. When he turned to her with Apollo between them, she felt as if something big was going to happen. Something that neither of them could take back.

The urge to stop him was strong, but she held herself back, waiting to see what he wanted to say.

"Olivia, you are the only woman I've ever met who has made me second guess what I want out of life." There was such an earnestness in his tone that Olivia found she could barely even breathe, let alone talk. So she just nodded once, acknowledging his confession. "I'll admit that I'm probably more terrified of this decision than I am of just about anything else I've done in my life, but it's worth it because walking away from whatever this is between us is unthinkable."

Olivia let out the breath she'd been holding and had to blink back tears. She hadn't even let herself consider that he might change his mind about leaving Christmas Grove. In her experience, people usually didn't change up their lives for someone else. But now this lovely man had spent an entire day doing her favors to maintain the inn. He'd taken to her dog as if Apollo were his own. Declan was such a devoted family man that he'd worked at Olivia's inn just so that his sister would still have a job when she was ready to go back to work.

To say that his love language was service to those he cared about was an understatement.

"You're a rare being, Declan. Do you know that about yourself?" she asked.

He scoffed. "There's nothing rare about me. I'm just a guy who likes to cook and is pretty good at it."

"You're a man who takes care of everyone around you. All the people you care about at least. You're kind, conscientious, and full of love to give. Did you know I saw all of that in you back when we met in San Francisco?"

His eyes glittered with trouble. "I thought that week was about something else entirely."

She felt her face flush. "It started out that way, yes. But did you ever figure out why I was gone so early that last day?"

"I figured you weren't one for awkward goodbyes," he said flippantly.

It was her turn to scoff. "Awkward isn't something I'm afraid of. However, being faced with saying goodbye to the kindest, most loving man I'd ever met was more than I could handle. So I left before I had to."

"That's why you didn't say goodbye?" He reached across Apollo and cupped her cheek. "Do you have any idea how disappointed I was when I woke up to find you gone that morning?" She shook her head and then leaned into his touch as he continued. "I almost went downstairs to pay the doorman to do whatever it would take to find out where you went. But that went against our pact, so I didn't. Imagine my surprise when I found you here in my sister's new hometown, needing a chef, no less."

"You didn't want to work for me at first," she insisted.

"That's because I wanted to sleep with you." He grinned.

Olivia's face flushed with heat. "Well, that's honest, I suppose."

He dropped his hand and slipped his fingers through hers. "I promise to always be honest with you. I can't guarantee that things will always be smooth sailing, but I'll never lie to you."

If Olivia's heart hadn't melted before, it did then. This was what she'd wanted. It didn't really have to do with a job or how driven her partner was or what town they lived in. It was this intimacy she had with Declan that she'd craved. The idea that they'd care for each other, consider each other, and together find a way to follow their dreams.

Declan had proven that he'd be willing to give up something he thought he wanted to be closer to her. But if the restaurant didn't work out and he had to leave to go work somewhere else, she felt like they could work it out. She'd hire someone to run the inn and go with him. Or try traveling back and forth. Literally anything other than just throwing their hands up and deciding it wasn't worth it.

Because he was. And she was damned sure she was, too.

"That's a promise I'll make to you, too, Declan. I'll always be honest about what's going on with me. I won't make you guess. And together, we'll get through whatever is thrown at us."

Declan tugged her gently, moving her toward him until their lips met. She kissed him earnestly, pouring all of her emotion into their connection, making sure he knew just how much she cared for him through that one innocent kiss.

When they pulled apart, he gave her a slow smile. "So I guess we're in this thing?"

"We're in this thing," she agreed and then smirked as she added, "I'm not sure you had to buy my dad's restaurant just to get the girl, but it was a really good gesture."

"Nothing's worth doing that isn't worth overdoing," he said and then leaned in for another kiss.

Olivia could've stayed there on her couch all night making out with Declan. But two things interrupted her. The first was Apollo, who was starting to think of Declan as his. Olivia had to bribe him off the couch with a treat just so Declan could get up. The second was when her phone buzzed with a Facetime call.

She grabbed her phone and then let out a gasp when she saw the name.

"Who is it?" Declan asked from the kitchen where he was pouring them more wine.

"Priscilla. I can't imagine what she wants."

"Answer it." Declan handed her a fresh glass of wine and then went to stand next to her so they could both chat with the movie star.

Olivia swiped to answer the phone, fully expecting it to be a butt dial, but when the screen came on, Priscilla and Leo were standing together, their faces in the frame.

"Olivia! Hi!" Priscilla said as if she were calling a long-lost friend instead of the woman she'd tortured for the last month.

Leo waved, grinning from ear to ear.

"Hey guys," Olivia said at the same time Declan said, "Where did you two run off to?"

"Washington," Leo called just before he dropped out of the frame.

Declan glanced at Olivia and back at Priscilla. He grinned at the movie star and said, "Looks like you're a long way from Hollywood."

"I definitely am. Leo and I are in Befana Bay, and I just wanted to show Olivia something."

"Oh yeah, what's that?" Olivia asked.

Priscilla's eyes sparkled as she flipped the phone and asked, "Does this look familiar?"

The phone panned, showing the lovely two-story house that sat above the Hood Canal and had a gorgeous view of the Olympic Peninsula. The sun was shining, but there were clouds on the horizon that made for a dramatic skyline.

"Looks a lot like a house I saw in a dream once," Olivia said.

The screen on the phone flipped around and Priscilla was back, her face shining with emotion. "Yeah. I saw it in a dream once before, too."

They shared a knowing look, both of them a little misty-eyed.

Priscilla was the first to look away as she cleared her throat and then said, "I really just wanted to thank you. If I hadn't seen my life and the future through fresh eyes, I would've missed out on something that I truly thought was never possible for me."

"I don't even know that I can take credit for that," Olivia said. She'd done some thinking and determined that maybe the magic that had allowed her to be Priscilla's guide in her dreams was magic from the inn. Lizzie had hinted that other ghosts lived at the inn. Maybe they'd been the guides. "Let's just chalk it up to the magic of The Enchanted."

"Okay. If you say so. There are a couple others here who want to say hi, too," Priscilla said and then turned the phone around so that it was trained on Tater and Scooter. The two pups immediately started jumping up and down when they spotted Olivia on the screen.

"Hey, you two. I hope you're being good for your mama. She has a few changes coming. Good ones, but changes all the same. So be kind, okay?"

They yelped and pawed at the phone, making their excitement known.

"Speaking of changes," Priscilla said, taking charge again. "Leo and I have a favor to ask."

Uh-oh. Olivia wasn't sure she wanted to hear it. After all the things Priscilla had demanded during her stay at the inn, it could be just about anything, and Olivia was too tired to speculate.

"What's the favor?" Declan asked. Sure, he wasn't afraid. He wasn't the one who'd had to clean her hair from the drain.

"Leo proposed this morning, and I said yes." She flashed a ring that dwarfed her small hand, nearly blinding Olivia when the sun hit it.

"It's gorgeous... I think," Olivia said. "Can't wait to see it in person someday if you guys ever come back here."

"That's the thing," Priscilla said. "We do want to come back. On New Year's Eve. We'd like to get married at midnight in the garden if it's not too late notice."

"The garden doesn't have any flowers," Olivia said stupidly. Of course it didn't. It was December, and there was snow on the ground most days.

"I'm pretty sure we can remedy that if we call a florist," Priscilla reasoned. "But we'd have to do it soon. It's just a few days until Christmas, and I'm sure if we don't get the ball rolling now, I'll likely end up holding red carnations from the grocery store."

"Of course. Yes," Olivia said, finally coming out of her shocked haze. "Since the inn was booked for the movie, I never took any other reservations. We're totally free. Invite whoever you want, but please check with me on the room situation. We don't want anyone sleeping in the hallways with Lizzie."

"Well, if they do, maybe Lizzie has some lessons for them too." Priscilla grinned. "Declan, are you still there?"

"Present," he said from his spot at the sink where he'd started rinsing dishes. Holy crow, the man was a saint, wasn't he?

"Can you do the catering? We'll pay whatever your rate is."

"Sure. Just send me a list of how many people and if there's anything special you want or don't want. I'll also make sure there are vegan options."

"You're the best." She blew him an air kiss. "Now let me talk to Apollo."

Olivia giggled while Priscilla gave Apollo all kinds of instructions that he completely ignored until she got to the one about making sure to give his mommy plenty of kisses. He looked over at Olivia and stuck his tongue out as if blowing her his version of a kiss. "Good boy, Apollo. Good boy."

Olivia asked her a few more questions about the wedding until suddenly, Priscilla said, "Gotta go. There are orcas swimming by the house."

The screen went blank, and Olivia stared at it as if she wasn't quite sure what had just happened.

Declan came and took the phone from her hand and put it on the counter. "I know that seemed weird and a complete one-eighty from her personality when she was on set, but at least we now know that Leo wasn't insane for falling for her."

"Orcas were swimming by the house, Declan," Olivia said, shaking her head in disbelief. "Are they in some sort of utopian wonderland?"

"Maybe so. But then, so are we." He hugged her, and when she finally wrapped her arms around him, he said, "Oh yeah. I forgot to tell you that I'm considering naming the restaurant Apollo's. What do you think?"

She pulled back abruptly, stared at him in complete shock, and then said, "You're something else, Declan McCabe. What do I think? I love it. It's perfect."

CHAPTER 28

"*I* wish I could help you," Payton said from her spot in a recliner in her living room.

"I already told you we don't need your help, sis," Declan said as he handed her a glass of wine.

He and Payton had invited Olivia over so that they could make her dinner, but since Payton was still in recovery all she did was help Olivia drink the wine. Declan was the one who'd cooked and cleaned up. It was the least he could do, considering the other two were busy planning the menu for Priscilla and Leo's wedding.

It turned out the women in his life had a lot of opinions on wedding food. He was happy to let them have at it while he took care of their culinary needs.

"Thank you, Declan," his sister said as she took a sip of her wine.

Olivia smiled up at him and lifted her face for a quick kiss before he retreated back to the kitchen to finish cleaning up. He'd made lasagna and garlic bread for his two best girls and still had to clean the pan. He glanced down at Apollo, who was at his feet, desperate for any scraps. "No lasagna for you, boy. But there is a treat in it for you if you hold out until I'm finished here."

Apollo flopped down right there on the floor at Declan's feet, willing to wait as long as it took.

Declan shook his head and got to work. After he was done cleaning up and was giving Apollo his treat, Declan heard some voices on the television, and then Olivia cried out, "No. Oh no. Where did that come from?"

"What's going on?" Declan asked when he stepped back into the living room.

Olivia just pointed at the television.

A woman in a bright yellow puffy jacket was on the local news, waving a gossip magazine and ranting about trash being sold in our stores.

"Isn't that Lemon Pepperson?" Declan asked. "What's she doing ranting about celebrity magazines on the local news?"

"Declan," Payton said, "I think you need to sit down."

He slowly lowered himself onto the couch next to Olivia and watched as the gossip rag was flashed on the screen.

"Oh my goddess, they are showing that horrible picture again," Olivia said. She had her hands covering her face and was peeking out between her open fingers.

Declan peered at the magazine cover on the screen. Olivia had her hair pulled up into a bun and there was a streak of... Was that green icing on her face? She looked flushed and not at all happy. "Where did they get that picture?" he asked absently, still trying to read the headlines.

All he saw was *CHEATING AND INTIMATE COFFEE DATES* stamped across the top of the gossip rag.

"It was taken at the bakeoff," Olivia said miserably. "The promo for the show started today. I look like a complete fool. Flour all over me, my face sweaty, and that streak of green icing. I look like I got into a fight with a five-year-old and lost."

"They're just trying to make you look frantic for ratings," Payton soothed. "Don't worry about the show. I'm sure they'll show you being just as lovely as you always are."

"I don't know if I was lovely that day. I was late, had no idea I was supposed to be there for hair and makeup, and then I burned the cookies. Everyone else looked so put together. I was a hot mess."

"Sounds like the makings of a star," Payton teased.

Olivia let out a huff of humorless laughter before turning her attention back to the report. "What are they saying?"

Declan cleared his throat. "It sounds like you and I are being blamed for breaking up the Hollywood sweethearts Leo West and Priscilla Cain."

"What? They aren't broken up," Olivia said. "I just talked to Priscilla a couple of hours ago. They're on their way up into the mountains for a few days before Christmas to have a little rest before everything really ramps up. First Christmas, then they'll be here to tie the knot. It's a lot to deal with."

"This breaking news says so." Declan couldn't keep the disgust out of his tone. He despised gossip rags just as much as he'd despised the *Letters to the Editor* column in his hometown. That's where everyone and their mother submitted their opinions about his parents when they were in a reckless phase. What he didn't understand was, if Priscilla and Leo were going strong, why were they being targeted? And why had they brought Olivia and him into it?

"I wouldn't worry about this," Payton said. "That magazine has been sued so many times for lies that I doubt they stay in business even a few months longer. Maybe it was a slow news day and this will all blow over by morning. It is just a local news station, after all."

"Yeah, maybe," Declan said, getting to his feet. "Olivia, are you ready to go? I'm tired and have a busy day tomorrow."

He saw his sister and Olivia exchange a worried glance.

"Stop looking at each other like I'm going to blow a gasket. We all know there's no truth to this news story. It will blow over."

"Right," Olivia agreed, looking cheerful. "Let's just go, and tomorrow we can start getting some of the rentals for the wedding."

"I'll call you about the rest of the menu details," Payton told Olivia.

Declan kissed his sister on the cheek, scooped up Apollo, and waited for Olivia to walk out the door before him.

As soon as they opened the door, camera lights flashed in their faces, blinding them.

"Is it true, Declan? Did you sleep with Priscilla Cain?"

"Olivia! Olivia! Is Leo West as dreamy naked as he is in all his clothes?"

More inappropriate questions were hurled at them

while more lights flashed in their faces. Apollo growled and even lunged for one of the photographers, but he missed. Fortunately for him, but it was too bad the vulture photographer got to keep his hand. If he tried touching Apollo again, Declan was going to punch him.

Once they were safely in Declan's truck, Olivia took Apollo off Declan's hands and secured him safely into his doggie bed in the back and then said, "Go. Let's get out of here."

Declan did as she asked and cursed under his breath when two of the cars followed them. One got so close it nearly tapped their bumper.

"Holy crow!" Olivia was turned around backward in her seat, staring at the two cars pursuing them. "This is ridiculous. They aren't going to find a story here," she insisted.

"I know," Declan said. "Hold on. I'm going to lose them."

Olivia reached up for the handle on the ceiling and said, "Do it. I'm ready."

He pressed on the gas, nearly running two red lights before he took a left and then a right and then a left again. His foot was heavy on the pedal as he pushed his truck as fast as it could go until they were outside the gates of the inn and suddenly surrounded by more photographers. He let out a frustrated growl. Usually Olivia kept the gates open, but since she didn't have any guests booked and no one was going to be there, she'd decided to close them. It was a good thing, too, because if they'd gotten back to an army of reporters on her front step, there was no telling what Declan would've done.

"What the hell?" Olivia cried when she saw them. "Bastards. I'm going to open the gate on the count of three," Olivia said. "Once we get through and into the house, I'll call the Christmas Grove police to see if there's anything we can do to get rid of them, and then we can make an official statement."

"You can. I'm not," Declan insisted. "I have nothing to say to those vultures."

"That's fine," Olivia said. "I will speak for both of us. You never have to say a word. Should we go in now?"

He gave her a quick nod and she counted down from three. When she got to one, the gates opened and as soon as they were through, they started to close again. Olivia watched as one of them tried to squeeze past the gates. When he got stuck, she took her phone out and flashed a variety of pictures. "That jackass is going to pay for that."

When Declan parked the truck in front of the inn, he glanced back and was relieved that they couldn't see the commotion at the road. At least if the reporters were going to stalk them for photos, they'd have to do it at a distance.

"Let's go in," he said.

Olivia nodded, looking stunned.

He knew the feeling. Once he was out of the truck, he rescued Apollo from the back seat and the three of them slipped into Enchanted, the very peaceful, very beautiful inn. Everything about it was worlds away from what was happening outside at the road. It almost seemed surreal.

Olivia led the way into her apartment and then grabbed her phone first thing to start making phone calls.

Declan sat at her desk and used her laptop to research

what was actually being said. The article that had been run was mostly vague. But the gist of it was that Priscilla and Leo were on the verge of getting engaged when Priscilla took a liking to a younger man and the inn owner seduced Leo West.

"Disgusting," Declan said as he slammed the laptop closed.

"Do I want to know what it says?" Olivia asked him, looking worried.

"No. It's sexist garbage, making it sound like both you and Priscilla are instigators of the supposed cheating."

"With each other?" she asked, looking horrified.

"No," he said, mustering the first chuckle since the story broke. "Neither of you could keep your hands to yourselves, apparently. Us poor men folk just didn't know what hit us."

"Vile." She picked up her phone and called someone. "Come on, Priscilla, pick up."

"Aren't she and Leo in the mountains? Will they even have cell reception?"

"Ugh!" She tossed the phone down and flopped down onto the floor with Apollo. "Now what? I already issued a statement to the local television and the newspaper, vehemently denying cheating, infidelity, or betrayal of any kind."

"I think that's all we can do," he said, sounding tired. "Commenting more will just further the news story, right?"

"Right."

They got ready for bed in silence, each of them processing what had happened. When they climbed into bed, Declan put Apollo between them and the dog immediately rolled over onto his back, demanding his belly rubs. Declan chuckled. "I knew I could count on you for some levity, buddy. Never change, okay?" he said to the dog as he rubbed his belly, making Apollo whine with happiness.

"I can't believe you two," Olivia said. "I'm going to need to get another dog just so there's a spare for me to love on."

"Nah. Apollo can handle both of us," Declan said, even as he rolled over onto his back and stared at the ceiling, trying to fight off the flight response that had been nagging at him from the moment he'd heard the bogus story on the news.

After Olivia gave Apollo a bunch of love, she rolled over and turned out the light.

Declan didn't say anything. He just lay there, watching the shadows on the walls.

"Are you okay?" she asked him.

"Yeah. Fine."

There was silence in the room until finally, Olivia said, "Promise me something?"

"I'll try," he said automatically, but at the moment, he didn't think he was capable of making any promises at all. The crushing weight of shame from the town gossip when he'd been a kid was crawling all over him. He knew it was irrational. That had nothing to do with what was happening now. He wasn't a kid, and his reputation wasn't going to be shot over a gossip magazine. Especially when the world learned that Priscilla and Leo were getting married at the inn just a week later.

There wasn't a scandal here, but that didn't mean the

vultures wouldn't do everything in their power to make it one.

"Promise me that no matter what happens, you'll be here for Christmas Eve."

"I'll do everything in my power to be here on Christmas Eve," he promised.

Olivia reached over Apollo and squeezed his hand. Then she rolled over the other way and went to sleep.

Declan spent the next several hours staring at the ceiling.

CHAPTER 29

*O*livia wasn't surprised to wake and find Declan missing from her bed. She'd had a feeling the night before that he'd bolt. It was as obvious to her as day and night that he was struggling with the bogus story. She also knew it had nothing to do with the story itself. It was the attention it was garnering.

Resigned, Olivia got up, took Apollo out, and went about her morning business, praying that Declan would reappear once he'd had time to think. But as the day wore on and she didn't hear from him, she stopped expecting to see him.

She spoke with Payton a few times and made plans to pick her up the following day so that she could spent Christmas Eve at the inn with Olivia and Declan if he happened to reappear. Neither of them were terribly hopeful.

She tried Priscilla a couple of times, but still only managed to get her voice mail. It wasn't that she thought

Priscilla could stop the bogus story from running, she just thought that maybe the star might have some insight on how to handle it.

The one time Olivia made it into town to pick up a few things at the store, she'd been the subject of whispers, pity, curiosity, and yes, derision. It was crazy how many people took stories like that at face value and never did any research to see if it was remotely true. It made her sick to her stomach, but it wasn't like she could do anything to change their perception. At one point when she was in the store, she wanted to shout that the story was false, that it was wild speculation. Or that it was just plain stupid.

But she didn't. She kept her head held high, purchased the items she needed for Christmas Eve dinner, and left without making a scene. She was both proud of herself and so angry she could spit. No wonder Declan had trauma from the gossip mill when he was a kid. People could be so cruel and thoughtless. As a kid, it would be doubly hard to navigate.

By the time Christmas Eve rolled around, the photographers at the end of her driveway had gone. It turned out that no one wanted to spend their holiday looking for another shot of Olivia ignoring them completely. No one wanted a shot like that. No, they wanted the one with green icing on her face and an expression of pure exhaustion so that they could interpret it however they wanted.

"Can I help you with anything?" Payton asked. "I can sit at the table and chop, slice, dice, or grate cheese. I don't need my foot for any of that."

"You're on." Olivia helped her chef to the dining room table, got her another chair for her leg, and then handed Payton a cutting board and a bunch of vegetables for their salad. Olivia had picked up filets for dinner, so she went to work on grilling them and making a batch of garlic mashed potatoes.

"You know what would make this evening perfect?" Payton said, trying hard to keep her spirits up. She was worried about Declan, too. They'd both called, and they'd both been ignored. Payton had finally texted him that she'd be at the inn with Olivia and that he should go there. But who knew if he would?

He'd promised Olivia he would try. And she was holding onto that. She had to. Otherwise, she'd start to think about how she'd almost had everything she'd ever wanted but then watched it all slip away when he left.

"What would make it perfect?" Olivia asked.

"Wine."

Olivia looked around, surprised that she hadn't yet opened a bottle. After rushing into the inn's kitchen to raid the stash, she came back with a very good, very expensive wine that she fully intended to drink to the last drop.

"This is excellent," Payton said after taking a sip.

"It is, isn't it? Declan chose it for Priscilla's wedding. I figure after the last few days, it's entirely justified that we drink as much as we want as long as we can still stumble into the wine closet."

Payton took another sip and giggled. "I like the way you think."

"Ahh, it's already working." Olivia poured herself a glass

and then set it aside. She wanted it, but she didn't want it until Declan showed up. She couldn't be two bottles in when he got there. Not today.

"I don't think he's coming," Payton said into her wine glass.

"I'm holding out hope," Olivia said. "I have to."

By the time they ate dinner, Payton was feeling no pain. The filets and potatoes were to die for, but the wine was clearly the star of the show for Payton.

As Olivia helped Payton to her room so that she could sleep it off, she was jealous. Maybe Olivia should've drank more. It certainly would've been less painful. Because her heart was breaking. She just knew that if Declan didn't show up that night, then whatever they'd had going was going to be shattered forever.

Olivia's trust would be broken, and she didn't know if they could come back from that.

With Payton tucked away in the nearest guest room, Olivia sat at the table next to the tree in the lobby with Apollo at her feet. All the lights were off except for the Christmas tree lights, leaving her mostly in darkness.

The vibe fit her mood. As she sat there, the angels on the tree started to sing "Silent Night." It was beautiful and haunting and nearly ripped her heart right out of her chest. But still, she sat there waiting. If she didn't get up, she didn't have to give up on Declan.

He'd promised.

She'd give him every opportunity to live up to his word.

As it got closer to midnight, the only sound was the ticking clock and the soft snore of Apollo, who was still at her feet but had given up on staying awake. If the clock struck midnight and Declan wasn't there, she'd head to bed. Christmas Eve would be over.

Five minutes.

Four minutes.

Three minutes.

Two

The inn's front door opened, and then she heard his voice. "Olivia?"

Tears filled her eyes, and she looked up to see the man she'd fallen for standing right in front of her, holding a small package that was wrapped in silver paper.

He immediately dropped to his knees and took both of her hands in his. "I wasn't sure I was going to make it."

"I knew you would," she said, her voice shaking.

He gave her a wobbly smile. "That's why we're a perfect match. Our belief in each other holds us both up."

She squeezed his hands, mostly just to assure herself that he was really there. That she wasn't imagining it. "Where did you go?"

"Everywhere. Nowhere. All I know is that when it was time to go home, my truck steered me here."

She cupped his cheeks and leaned in, giving him a slow, lingering kiss. "I missed that."

"I missed you." He handed her the box. "It's not much, but it means something to me."

She took the small box and stared at it, studying it until she lifted her gaze to his and asked, "Should I open it now?"

"Yes."

With shaking fingers, Olivia opened the small box and smiled through her happy tears. "It's a glass hummingbird."

"For your tree. I thought it would be nice to start a new tradition. One we can both contribute to."

"It's perfect," she said and stood. "Help me find a spot for it?"

Together they studied the tree, found a spot near the top, and hung the ornament. It immediately started to flutter its fragile wings, creating a beautiful kaleidoscope of color from the lights.

Olivia let out a happy laugh and leaned into Declan. "It's perfect. Thank you."

"You're welcome. I got something for Apollo too, but it's not nearly as interesting."

"If it goes in his mouth, he disagrees."

They both laughed and together with Apollo in Declan's arms, they went into her apartment and straight to the bedroom.

As Declan tucked Apollo into the small dog bed on Olivia's side of the bed, she spoke.

"I have to ask this just once."

He paused to look up at her. "Yes."

"You don't even know what the question is," she said, giving him a gentle smile.

"Yes, I do, and I'm staying. For good. It turns out that fear is a funny thing. Once you face it, it's not so fearful anymore."

Olivia wasn't exactly sure what that meant, but he sounded so confident, so sure of himself, that she didn't

A WITCH FOR MR. MISTLETOE

question him. Instead, she walked up to him and started to undo the buttons of her dress.

He watched for a moment and then gently knocked her hands away and trailed his fingers over her bare arms as he held her gaze. "It's been a long couple of days. I'd really like it if you'd let me unwrap the only present I really wanted for Christmas."

Olivia nodded as her entire body lit with anticipation. "Please, Declan. I've waited long enough, don't you think?"

"Too long," he corrected and then went to work, making her forget everything except his kisses, his touch, his love.

Long after they were done with their love-making, Olivia lay wide awake in his arms, brushing her fingertips over his muscular chest. "Declan?" she whispered.

"Yes, love?" His voice was raspy but soft and full of affection. It pleased her all the way down to her toes.

"What do you think about getting Apollo a girlfriend?"

"You mean you want him to sire puppies?" he asked, understanding her immediately.

"Yes."

"What would we do with them? Keep them?"

"Just one," she said sleepily. "That way there's one for each of us."

He chuckled. "That's going to be a lot of belly rubs."

"I'm up for the task," she said as she felt the soft tap of Apollo's paw on the side of the bed. She rolled over and found him asking to get up on the bed, so of course she obliged. As soon as she set him free, he ran over to Declan and curled up beside him. "See? I love him more than cheesecake, and this is what happens."

Declan laughed, kissed the top of her head, and said, "Yes. If Apollo sires a litter, I think we have more than enough room for one more puppy."

Olivia smiled into his chest, nodded, and said sleepily, "This is the best Christmas ever."

CHAPTER 30

*P*ayton McCabe sat in a chair at one of the reception tables and watched as her ridiculous brother walked around with a bundle of mistletoe, charging for kisses as if he were a mobile kissing booth.

"He's going to catch something. You know that, right?" Payton asked Olivia.

"Nah. No one really wants to kiss him except me. Everyone else is just giving him money and pretending to kiss his tipsy butt before pushing him away."

"Everyone except Lemon Pepperson. I think this is her third time back for a smooch," Payton pointed out.

Olivia wrinkled her nose at the other woman. "You might be right. I'll make sure he rinses extra well with mouthwash."

Payton threw her head back and laughed. She'd thought she couldn't love her boss more than she already had, but now that she was with Declan, Olivia was the sister she'd always wanted.

They were at Priscilla and Leo's wedding, and the mistletoe money was a fundraiser to help fix a failing bridge that connected the town to a gorgeous city-owned park.

After Priscilla and Leo returned to Christmas Grove for their wedding, they'd issued a forceful statement about the status of their relationship and admonished those who had accused Olivia and Declan of any involvement. It turned out that someone had taken Olivia's innocent answers to the questions about her relationship with Leo that the host of *The Great Christmas Grove Cookie Bakeoff* had asked and made up nonsense in order to sell papers.

Priscilla and Leo had demanded an apology from the gossip rag that ran the bogus story. From there the story really blew up, and now there was an investigation into the magazine that had ignored all journalistic integrity.

It turned out that Priscilla and Leo had wanted to do something with all the media attention their wedding had garnered, so they'd worked with the city to find out what projects needed money to be completed and had started a mistletoe challenge online. For each picture their supporters showed of them kissing someone under the mistletoe, Leo and Priscilla would donate a dollar up to a total of a million dollars. They were already more than halfway to their goal, and the challenge had only started the day before.

To help promote it, Declan was going around to all the guests, trying to get mistletoe pictures that they could post online with *#MrMistletoe*. And it was working, too, because more and more pictures were going up all over the internet.

Olivia sighed. "I think I need to go rescue him. Someone's great-aunt is looking to move in."

Payton chuckled and said, "Good luck. I'll likely be right here."

Olivia patted her on the arm and said, "Text me if you need more wine."

"Count on it." The wine was just as good that night as it had been on Christmas Eve. Ever since her brother had come to his senses and stopped running away, Payton had been overjoyed. She had her brother back for the first time in years. Sure, they'd always been close, but now Declan wasn't quite as broody and he joked more. It was really nice to see.

Now if Payton could just find her own man to date, then maybe she wouldn't feel like the third wheel all the time. It wasn't that she minded being alone. It was just hard when she had to watch her brother and Olivia swimming in their sea of happiness while Payton was stuck in her living room, waiting for her damned leg to heal.

Just three more weeks if everything went well. Three. More. Weeks.

She thought she'd die waiting.

"Hello, Payton," a man said as he sat right next to her and passed her a fresh glass of wine.

Payton jerked her head to the side, finding the most beautiful human she'd ever met casually talking to her as if he wasn't Atlas Mazer, the frontman for Mazer, the most successful rock band since the Beatles. She swallowed hard, trying not to stare at his angelic face, dark hair, and deep turquoise eyes. No doubt, he'd taken down stronger women than her with just one look. "Um, hello. How do you know my name?"

"How is it you don't know mine?" he asked.

She chuckled. "I'm behind on my pop culture studies?"

"No, you're not. I could tell you recognized me the moment I sat down. But I appreciate you trying to be cool about it."

"There was no trying. I'm just cool naturally," she said.

His eyes glittered. "I can see that. What do you do for a living, Payton?"

"I'm a chef. You?"

He chuckled. "We both know you know the answer to that, so let's not waste time."

She shrugged. "If you say so, but I still don't know how you knew my name."

His lips twitched as he drummed his fingers on the tabletop. "That really bothers you, doesn't it?"

"No." *Yes.* She just hated feeling like she was missing part of the conversation. Who had he talked to about her, and what had they said? But she wasn't going to ask this cocky musician. It seemed perfectly clear to Payton that if she didn't hold her cards close to the vest, this man was going to eat her alive. And she was going to let him.

She took a long sip of her wine. It really was delicious.

"I have a proposition for you, Payton," Atlas said. "Are you up for it?"

"I guess we won't know until you tell me what it is," she said, enjoying this banter more than she should. Why were cocky men always her downfall? If there was one within five miles, she was bound to sniff him out. Only this one had found her, hadn't he?

How much wine had she had to drink? One, two… three, four, five. Five. Yeah, that was it. No, six. Six glasses of wine.

Whoa. It was a good thing she wasn't supposed to be walking. She wasn't sure she could.

"Payton? Are you okay?" Atlas asked as if he'd been trying to get her attention.

"Yeah, fine. Just thinking about all the things I have to do tomorrow." She winced internally. WTF was that? Who was she, and how did she turn in her woman card?

Atlas stared at her, frowning for a long moment before he burst out laughing. "You're something else."

What did that mean exactly? Something else. Something else other than what? The drunk guy passed out in the raised flowerbeds out back?

"So, that proposal," Payton prompted. "What can I do for you?"

"Ah, that. I need a wife for a weekend," he said, sounding completely serious.

"Excuse me?" she asked, grateful she hadn't been drinking her wine. She didn't want to spit out an ounce of that stuff.

"Yeah, you know, a wife. Someone to take on business dinners, to buffer the family, to make sure I don't throw my wine in their faces."

"Oh no, Atlas, never waste wine like that. It would be an effing tragedy."

His grin widened. "See, I knew you knew my name."

Dammit! She hadn't meant to say it. She cleared her throat, hoping that it would somehow sober her up, but of course it didn't work. When she turned to get a full look at Atlas, her entire being screamed for her to do him this one favor.

"You want to help me. I can tell."

She rolled her eyes. "You're awfully sure of yourself."

"I have reason to be," he said matter-of-factly.

"Yeah, I suppose you do, but it's not going to be with me. Sorry. I'd consider it, but I broke my leg last month and—"

"When are you supposed to be walking again?" he asked.

"A few weeks."

"That timing works for me." He gave her a slow, seductive smile. A smile that said he knew what he was doing and wasn't ever going to stop until he got exactly what he wanted.

"I'll pay you half-a-million dollars to be my date to the family reunion and pretend to be my wife," he said, staring straight into her pale blue eyes. "What do you say?"

"I say half-a-million dollars is a lot of money. Why would you pay me when you could get practically anyone to do it for free?" Even as she played it cool, her heart was hammering against her ribcage. She'd be a fool to turn this down, wouldn't she?

"Because, Payton, none of the college girls who follow my band around are nearly as hot as you, and when Atlas Mazer walks in the room, he always walks in with the best. What do you say? Three days and I'll transfer 500K into your account."

Good goddess, that was a good line. How could she say

no to any of this? With that kind of money she could finally be financially secure. Never have to worry about paying a bill. Never wonder if there were layoffs coming if she was going to be the first to go. How hard could it be? "I'll tell you what, Atlas, you tell me how you knew my name and I'll do it."

His lips curved into a smile that resembled the Cheshire Cat as he pointed at her phone on the table. The phone that was in its monogrammed case.

"It's a deal then?" Atlas held his hand out.

"I'm a woman of my word." She shook his hand and then felt like a silly teenager when she didn't want to wash it. Atlas Mazer had sat down next to her, asked her to be his pretend wife, and offered her a half-million dollars for her trouble.

"Perfect," he said, standing and moving in closer to her. "I'll see you soon, wife. In the meantime, let me leave you with something to remember me by." Atlas dipped his head and without any warning, he claimed her lips and kissed her so thoroughly that when he stepped back, her head swam.

Atlas gave her a moment to catch her breath, and when she met his gaze, he said, "There's more where that came from, sweetheart. I'll be in touch."

DEANNA'S BOOK LIST

Witches of Keating Hollow:
Soul of the Witch
Heart of the Witch
Spirit of the Witch
Dreams of the Witch
Courage of the Witch
Love of the Witch
Power of the Witch
Essence of the Witch
Muse of the Witch
Vision of the Witch
Waking of the Witch
Honor of the Witch
Promise of the Witch

Witches of Christmas Grove:
A Witch For Mr. Holiday

A Witch For Mr. Christmas
A Witch For Mr. Winter
A Witch For Mr. Mistletoe
A Witch For Mr. Frost

Witches of Befana Bay:
The Witch's Silver Lining

Premonition Pointe Novels:
Witching For Grace
Witching For Hope
Witching For Joy
Witching For Clarity
Witching For Moxie
Witching For Kismet

Miss Matched Midlife Dating Agency:
Star-crossed Witch
Honor-bound Witch
Outmatched Witch
Moonstruck Witch

Jade Calhoun Novels:
Haunted on Bourbon Street
Witches of Bourbon Street
Demons of Bourbon Street
Angels of Bourbon Street
Shadows of Bourbon Street
Incubus of Bourbon Street
Bewitched on Bourbon Street

Hexed on Bourbon Street
Dragons of Bourbon Street

Pyper Rayne Novels:
Spirits, Stilettos, and a Silver Bustier
Spirits, Rock Stars, and a Midnight Chocolate Bar
Spirits, Beignets, and a Bayou Biker Gang
Spirits, Diamonds, and a Drive-thru Daiquiri Stand
Spirits, Spells, and Wedding Bells

Ida May Chronicles:
Witched To Death
Witch, Please
Stop Your Witchin'

Crescent City Fae Novels:
Influential Magic
Irresistible Magic
Intoxicating Magic

Last Witch Standing:
Bewitched by Moonlight
Soulless at Sunset
Bloodlust By Midnight
Bitten At Daybreak

Witch Island Brides:
The Wolf's New Year Bride
The Vampire's Last Dance
The Warlock's Enchanted Kiss

The Shifter's First Bite

Destiny Novels:
Defining Destiny

Accepting Fate

Wolves of the Rising Sun:
Jace

Aiden

Luc

Craved

Silas

Darien

Wren

Black Bear Outlaws:
Cyrus

Chase

Cole

Bayou Springs Alien Mail Order Brides:
Zeke

Gunn

Echo

ABOUT THE AUTHOR

New York Times and USA Today bestselling author, Deanna Chase, is a native Californian, who's splits her time between New Orleans and the Pacific Northwest. When she isn't writing, she is often goofing off with her husband, traveling with her besties, or playing with her two shih tzu dogs. For more information and updates on newest releases visit her website at deannachase.com.

Made in the USA
Thornton, CO
12/20/22 08:21:00